© Tina Turnbow

DAPHNE MERKIN

22 MINUTES OF
UNCONDITIONAL LOVE

DAPHNE MERKIN is the author of the novel *Enchantment*, which won the Edward Lewis Wallant Award for best novel on a Jewish theme, as well as two collections of essays and the memoir *This Close to Happy*. She is a former staff writer for *The New Yorker*, and her essays frequently appear in *The New York Times*, *Bookforum*, *The New Republic*, *Departures*, *Elle*, *Travel + Leisure*, *Tablet*, and many other publications. Merkin has taught writing at the 92nd Street Y, Marymount Manhattan College, and Hunter College, and she currently teaches in Columbia University's MFA program. She lives in New York City.

22 MINUTES OF UNCONDITIONAL LOVE

22 MINUTES OF UNCONDITIONAL LOVE

DAPHNE MERKIN

PICADOR

FARRAR, STRAUS AND GIROUX

NEW YORK

Picador
120 Broadway, New York 10271

Library of Congress Control Number: 2020934691
Picador Paperback ISBN: 978-1-250-79865-7

Designed by Gretchen Achilles
Interior art by Vesnin_Sergey / Shutterstock.com

Our books may be purchased in bulk for promotional, educational, or
business use. Please contact your local bookseller or the Macmillan Corporate
and Premium Sales Department at 1-800-221-7945, extension 5442,
or by email at MacmillanSpecialMarkets@macmillan.com.

Picador® is a U.S. registered trademark and is used by Macmillan Publishing Group,
LLC, under license from Pan Books Limited.

For book club information, please visit facebook.com/picadorbookclub or
email marketing@picadorusa.com.

picadorusa.com • instagram.com/picador
twitter.com/picadorusa • facebook.com/picadorusa

1   3   5   7   9   10   8   6   4   2

To Zoë, my North Star

Il y a toujours quelque chose d'absent qui me tourmente.

—CAMILLE CLAUDEL,
In a letter to Auguste Rodin, 1886

I am a searcher . . . I always was . . . and I still am . . .
searching for the missing piece.

—LOUISE BOURGEOIS

22 MINUTES OF UNCONDITIONAL LOVE

In this story there is no final scene, no decisive change of heart or firm resolve so much as a furious inner struggle—a struggle that has left no discernible traces yet has marked me as surely as bruises after a fall. Because there is no end to the hunger for unconditional love and no end to my belief that he was the one to give it to me. I have no stopwatch to measure how long the experience of sexual pleasure—of losing yourself—lasts at any particular time: it could be ten minutes, or fifteen, or twenty-two. How do you measure the crest of a wave? All I know is that when it vanishes, it leaves in its wake a devouring appetite for more.

To this day I can't forget how he was always touching me in bed, acting as though my skin came as a surprise. "You feel so soft," he said. "So smooth." Nothing very original in that, I realize, and yet coming from him I felt it as a lovely succumbing, a weakening of his ordinary resistance.

Then there is this: I am a writer, a believer in the powers of art to shape experience so that others might recognize something of themselves in it. Except when it comes to my own life, it appears. I have decided to tell this story now, after all these years, as a way of forcing it to the finish line. I am still confused about how I got to that place to begin with and how I got out without going mad, howling like a wolf. I think it had something to do, despite all evidence to the contrary, with some intact shred of a life force. I willed him out of my life in order to pursue a more sane existence, one that would include a husband and children—a daughter I would bring up to feel full in herself, without vast absences or ravaging needs. But it was just that: an effort of will rather than a natural ending—only a sense that if I wanted to survive, I would have to move on.

Meanwhile, the efficient little clock on my desk keeps marking the passage of time. If you pick up this clock—a practically weightless black Braun traveling clock, with white hour and minute hands and a yellow second hand—and hold it close to your ear, you can hear a faint, even tick. So many days, months, and years have intervened, not to mention a marriage, the daughter I wished for, and another child on the way, you'd think he'd have no place in my thoughts anymore. And for periods of time he doesn't, only to alight on my nerve endings once again. It has to do, I imagine, with the tedium, the worn routines that are an inescapable part of domestic life. Some habit of my husband's that I have tired of, such as the way he blinks his eyes rapidly when someone disagrees with him. Or the way my daughter puts up an argument about something perfectly reasonable, like getting into her pajamas before bedtime.

Suddenly a space opens up, a wedge of restlessness mixed with longing, and Howard Rose walks back in.

PROLOGUE

IN THE BEGINNING we kissed: everyone kisses in the beginning. It was only later that the other stuff came welling up between us like blood. Only later that I crouched on his bed on all fours, his finger inside me—inside my "vadge-eye-nah," as my daughter, Sarah, calls it proudly, syllable by syllable, befitting a child of these demystifying times—his mouth biting through mine as though it were a piece of fudge.

His mouth was arguably his best feature, especially in repose, when it looked sensuous—the lips full and curvy, made for kissing. But everything changed when he smiled. I should explain that he had several different kinds of smiles: There was the half-smile when he was amused, receptive to the comic possibilities inherent in a given situation. Then there was his official pleased-as-punch smile, which made the whole lower half of his face recede and struck me as oddly sheepish. The smile I liked least was the one that spoke of nothing good, flickering across his face when he was about to be cruel.

I still have the piece of paper, torn from a notebook, on which I faithfully recorded—ever the writer, even before I actually stepped into the role, duty bound to police experience, to pin it down and handcuff it—his impression of my breasts. *Luscious handfuls*, he told me. I've been meaning to write this book for years; sometimes I feel as though I've been carrying it around like a hump on my back, a hump no one can see. If I could keep myself from writing it, I probably would, but the truth is I can't anymore. It's the kind of tale I keep hoping to find already told by someone else, someone else with an invisible hump weighing her down until she can no longer stand it and hurls it off her and out into the world. But all I've read are fragments scattered here and there—a couple of pages buried in a novel, a paragraph or two in a memoir, pieces of the story, allusions but never the whole shebang.

And yet I know deep in my bones that this experience, this skewed impulse toward connection that lies somewhere between passion and annihilation, between fusion and combustion, is not mine alone. That it earmarks other women, those looking to affirm themselves through a man's eyes and toward which end they will do almost anything. Some of the details contained herein I've been afraid to admit to myself; others I've been afraid to admit to anyone *but* myself. Then there's my sense that I'm not supposed to be the kind of woman this happens to . . . all of which has made for difficulties, reasons to do other things than write this book.

But now that I find myself pregnant again—the beginnings

of a new life stirring within me, cementing my bond with my husband, Richard, ever more conclusively, at least from the outside in, hemming me into one way of life rather than another—I feel I must tell my story. I must write it down before it becomes too shadowy, a mere prelude to the main act of life in which I now reside, when the truth is that everything that has come all these years later often seems like a denouement. It's for myself, of course, that I tell it, but also for all of you who have stumbled into this kind of twisted love—love indistinct from madness—and reeled from its force. The way it threatens to destroy you but also to infuse you with something vital, a feeling of completeness, an end to the never-ending struggle of being a person alone on the planet, separate inside your own skin rather than merged with someone else.

Obsession makes for good copy, they say. But what kind of *life* does obsession make for, that's the real question. And even more important: What kind of life do you live *after* you've given it up? Is it like being in a room with the lights turned permanently low—a less intense atmosphere that reminds you by its very pallor of the brightness you've lost? How sustaining, that is, are memories of passion, of erotic immersion? Can they last you a lifetime? Can you draw upon them at night in bed—his mouth bearing down on yours, his tongue or finger inside you the better to slick you up into a state of readiness—when you are sleeping next to a man you've never been obsessed with but who is all the same the man you've chosen to be with over the long haul? Or do these memories eventually fade, like worn-out stars?

Then there is also this: How do you give up something that's nestled in your marrow, this particular taste in loving, one that is crisscrossed with hate, with specks of long-ago humiliations endured but never forgotten? What I'm referring to is an appetite for a certain degree of debasement, being reduced to a panting, abject creature in the name of sexual pleasure. The fine-tuning of relative power that naturally obtains between couples pitched way up into the insistent blare of one who dominates and one who submits.

Everything, even styles of love, begins way back, in some dim corner of a memory or a sensation that has been stored without your even knowing it. I do believe there is an inherent etiology to these things—an original imprinting that eventually hardens into a pattern that seems inexorable. You don't have to be a die-hard Freudian or even a believer in the unconscious, merely someone who keeps going back to the same dry well, the same original absence, to subscribe to a retrospective theory of origins: we become as we were fated to be. All this talk about the plasticity of the brain notwithstanding, how many of us change our stripes past the formative years of childhood, become unrecognizable to ourselves and others? Shape-shifters are the stuff of science fiction; in real life we are stuck with the given color of our eyes, the influences that mark us, all that goes right—or, as it may be, wrong.

I, for instance, began as a lonely, watchful little girl, ever on the lookout for turns in the wind, changes without warning. My family lived in Hastings-on-Hudson, in a mock-Tudor house with a carpeted den and three bathrooms, one of which was designated as a "guest" bathroom. I remember from an early age wanting to be someone other than myself, a girl who looked and felt differently than I did, one who had different parents—a mother who said "darling" when I came in the door or a father who attended my dance recitals, or who knew the names of my friends. On the occasions my mother came to open school days, she sat in the back next to the other, uniformly excited parents, looking bored. I noticed anxiously she hadn't bothered to dress up like most of the other mothers had.

My mother worked as a buyer for women's sportswear at Saks. She favored me in unadorned dresses and in simple, boyish clothes—jeans and T-shirts—when I was young enough to comply with her wishes. I had little say in my choice of wardrobe, as in most things. As I grew older and showed signs of having a will of my own, when she was angered by something I said or did, she would not acknowledge me. I would become desperate and I sometimes think that this early experience of desperation weakened me, left me without a psychological spine, made me susceptible to the imposition of someone else's will.

My father was a practical man, a doctor who worked at a local hospital and who disappeared most weekends into his woodworking shop in the basement, where he painstakingly banged out objects for the house—a table, a cabinet or bookcase. By the age of nine or ten I began wondering whether he would have been more interested in me if I were a boy, like my cousin Alex. He liked to show Alex things, the correct way to throw a baseball or hold a bat, those kinds of male diversions. Or if I had been a girl more like my sister, Rebecca, athletic and outgoing, instead of a bookish type. He had liked coaching Rebecca, who was an excellent swimmer, when she competed in races at the community pool.

My father was good-looking—he had a full head of hair and blazing blue eyes—and would have been even better-looking if he had been a bit taller. But then, I hadn't been aware that he was short—relatively short, five eight or five nine—until a friend mentioned it to me in passing, an obvious detail one seemingly couldn't overlook. And yet I did: My father, short? As a child I saw him as a towering figure, someone who couldn't be scaled by someone as small as I was. I have never really revamped this image and have thus remained blind to the physically unimposing reality of him, blind to my enlargement of his presence.

In any case, I experienced myself as insufficiently compelling, missing a crucial dimension that would have made me lovable, a cherished object of parental affection. I accumulated a secret stash of self-hatred to explain my parents' bewildering lack of interest, reasons to find myself undeserving, whether it was the too-thick shape of my eyebrows or my tendency to burst into tears at the smallest provocation. As a result I became—have become—a person who is always looking to fill out the internal picture I have of myself, who thinks that someone or something else might complete me, make me worthy of notice. If I could have changed places with my sister, who seemed mysteriously unbothered by my parents—resilience is the name they give this trait these days—I would have.

This isn't to say that I have a weak or malleable personality but that I can't figure out who I am—what my psychological net value is, so to speak, particularly when it comes to men. I can't figure out, to be specific, what sexual pleasure consists of without invoking the principle of power. Someone is up, someone is down, someone is being made to do another's bidding. The Germans, leave it to them, have a word for this sort of inclination: *Hörigkeit*, they call it. Sexual dependence or abjection.

In these kinds of lovestruck stories the man in question is never really interesting. No one found Howard Rose interesting—no one, that is, but me. I'm not sure I found him interesting either, not in any clear sense, so much as a reminder of where I emotionally began and would always remain, no matter how hard I tried to move away: Dazzled by intermittency, by the light beaming on and then off, a glimpse of absolute happiness followed by nothing but the lonely darkness. The allure of remoteness, affection edged in ice and always on the verge of melting away, of disappearing entirely. Suggesting a greater possibility of being converted into love than all the tender kisses in the world.

To me, then, he was someone I had tried to win over long ago and had succeeded for a while, only to fail in the end—or, more exactly, only to realize that what I longed for would eventually leave me in tatters. He was my mother, I suppose, with bits and pieces of my father thrown in, but to what extent that clarifies matters is anyone's guess. How everything conspires to keep us in the dark about ourselves.

If I write all this down, put it into the third person and pretend it happened to someone else, someone I happen to know intimately, will it change anything, redeem what seems irredeemable by putting a fictional gloss on it? Will it transform these doings from one woman's plight into something larger, a case history with application to others—to you, the reader, for instance? Who, I might add, wants to read a story, even one promising some juicy sex, if it isn't about you, too? Like going into a store ready to spend money only to be peered at by some frosty saleswoman and told, "Sorry, we have nothing in your size." How maddening. You open a book (when you could, after all, be doing so many other things: catching up on your email, watching TV, skimming a magazine, reading a different book, making love, going to a yoga or exercise class, masturbating, cutting onions, eating, drinking, shopping, so many other things) expecting exactly that—to find something in your size: so I hereby give you Judith Stone, a woman with an ache coursing through her, who is me, who is you, or might very well be you.

Who knows, finally, by what process an obsession begins to take hold: begins, by stealth, to fill in a gaping hole you didn't even know was there. It seems to me now, all these years later, that I wanted him forever almost within minutes of meeting him. But why? The randomness of it still gnaws at me. I suppose those who study such processes would point to the crackle of human electricity: a potent pheromone, or a clamor starting up in one's limbic system, sending out neurons of desire. I myself believe none of it. Better you should ask: Why is the sky blue?

I should mention that I am not reducible merely to my obsession, although it has taken up so much space in my mind. It's not as though you'd be able to point me out as a woman who long ago rose to the siren call of submission; there's nothing about me that's a dead giveaway, no clear sign that I've been places most civilized people—or people who consider themselves civilized—haven't gone. But there never is in these matters, is there? You would pass me in the street and nothing about me—not my midlength chestnut hair, nor the angle of my jawline, not even what I've been told is my direct gray-eyed gaze—would lead you to surmise that I am a woman who once gave herself over to a certain kind of erotic compliance.

It's been years since I've harkened to the insistent tom-tom beat of this particular mating call, the way I walked around with nothing between myself and the air I breathed but visions of him, his dry laugh, his hands, the feel of him moving inside me, watching me with narrowed eyes, him, him, him. The sex itself was no different in the end from other sex but singular enough to keep me fixated on the memory of his going inside me, deeper, it seemed, than other men had ventured, breaking and entering my body, slowly, then faster, then pulling halfway out, then charging back in, me getting wetter, him getting harder and more forceful, the closest I'd come to an experience of losing myself than any I'd known.

I liked putting his penis—no whopper, but a pleasing length and width—in my mouth, which was not an activity I had been overly fond of before. There was something about the tangy taste of him that reminded me of the way a stalk of grass tastes when you suck on it. I see myself bent over him as he sits pasha-like on a couch, my hair tumbled forward, concentrating on pleasing him. I see myself, that is, watching me bent over him as seen through his eyes, the servicing female on her knees. A double voyeurism; who is behind the camera, directing, him or me? And isn't part of the thrill that at some point you can't tell any longer? Then, too, he spent a lot of time on my breasts, stroking them, sucking on my nipples, making them stand up straight as soldiers as I reached down to hold his stiffened penis.

Already at the beginning I felt how necessary this was to me, this dialogue between bodies, so different from the endless attempts to connect by way of words. I always knew when he was about to come because he would grind his teeth, as though gearing himself up to win the race that lay ahead. He complained that I didn't make enough noise in bed, but I thought he had these inane ideas about women's wild screaming and moaning from the movies. How could I explain that arousal made me silent and intent, just as it made him, and that this was how it was meant to be, far from the jangle of the street, in an apartment in a sleeping city.

Astonishing, when you think about it, the weight some of us give to sex, treating it as transformational when the reality is it leaves nothing in its wake but the flickering memory of pleasure. If you asked me why I was willing to pay the price for his kind of love, love tantamount to possession, I would ask you what's so great about autonomy. Autonomy is taxing, is you being on your own, when what I'm always looking for is the buffer of another person, a way to muffle my sniping inner chatter. I suppose there must be something in the middle, something between being starkly alone and being stuck together with someone else, like a pair of magnets, but I've never figured out what it is.

I recognize, of course, that this wish to merge oneself with another person probably derives from something that miscarried early on—a feeling of abandonment that keeps haunting you. Somewhere, someone didn't pay enough attention when you were young and open, or paid attention but at too high a tab—saying, in effect, I will give you what you need but only if you do as I say. After that, that kind of bargaining is in your blood; nothing that is sweet and wholehearted has much draw.

But what I also know to be true is this: When we were together, I was always on his mind. Never, for a moment, did he forget about me. I was sure of that; like a baby in its mother's womb, I was with him always. Now that it has all been over for so long, despite being a wife and mother I am on my own again, on no one's mind except as circumstance determines it. Sarah wants me when she wants me but forgets about me when she is playing with her dolls or is lost in one of those elaborate computer games where you build a house and decorate it and fill it with a family. Richard phones me at least once a day just to check in but he is also content to leave me to my own devices, especially now that I have given up editorial work for writing and can schedule my days as I see fit. I suppose this sort of independence is what passes in our advanced society for freedom.

But when I think about what it meant *not* to be free—the liberty of *un*freedom, that is, to be captive to the dictates of desire, however wayward—my whole body moves toward the memory, bringing me back and back and back, like a sailboat bobbing out endlessly to sea, past the waves, toward the far-off horizon.

I

"YOU FEEL SO *SOFT*," he whispers in her ear, slipping his hand inside the waistband of her pants and down under her cotton underwear. Now his hand is on the naked flesh of her ass, on her flesh, which is so soft. He circles a finger around her anus and then wiggles inside it.

"Do I," she says. No one has ever dared to do this to her before in public—in a movie theater, moreover—no one, that is, until Howard Rose. In the darkness around them she hears breathing and whispers, the crunching of popcorn, but she might as well be alone on a desert island with this man. She is wet, she drips wetness like a leak. She has known Howard Rose less than two weeks—ten days it must be—and already she is impaled on the end of his sexual spearing, trapped like a fly on sticky paper. She hasn't seen him for several days now, but it might as well be a Siberia of days, it's so cold without him.

The movie they are watching is lightweight to the point of disappearing, a comedy set in a country house in France. All the women in the film have long, tanned legs and on several occasions everyone gathers around a refectory table to eat delicious-looking stews that they mop up with crusty pieces of bread. She finds herself getting hungry just watching, and somehow this hunger morphs into a sexual hunger, a sensation of something dropping down deep inside her, creating a craving in her body.

"You're nice and wet," Howard Rose whispers, his breath smelling slightly of peppermint. "I want to fuck you right now."

He turns his head back to watch the movie. She stares at his profile, the leanness of his face, the blackness of his beard, and the incongruous lushness of his mouth. She is mortified and excited by the evidence of her senses, the stream that has started up between her legs, a steady stream of desire. Something in her is excited by his brazen impropriety, his disregard for the conventions of public behavior. The slight edge of contempt that underlies his daring excites her even more.

They leave the movie before it's over and take a taxi to Howard Rose's apartment. This is only her second time there and already she feels she's committed his one-bedroom to memory, will never be able to forget the way he drops his keys on the desk when he comes in, or the small half-circle of a dining table right off the kitchen, or the batik spread on his low bed. He takes his clothes off in a flash, first his pants and his Calvin Klein underpants (men's underpants, with their extra fold of cotton around the crotch, always put her in mind of diapers), then his sweater and shirt in one fell swoop over his head.

She sits on his brown fake-suede couch and watches his naked body appear in its sinewy yet fragile glory, a body that moves her in some way beyond the sexual, that makes her want to crush and be crushed at the same time. His thighs are long and taut and his penis is well sized and straight, set between full balls. She has come late to sexual activity, has imbibed her mother's stated disgust with the whole thing and still thinks of erotic pleasure as untrustworthy, but sometimes the untrustworthy has an added appeal.

"Come here," Howard Rose says. He has moved to his bedroom, where he lies under the covers, patting the space next to him, then folding his hands behind his head. "I think I know what you want."

"It's cold," she says, rubbing her arms, "or maybe I'm imagining it." Her voice gives her away; it is thick with longing. This is still at the beginning of their involvement, before she has fully learned how little he can tolerate anything but the most appreciative of responses. She doesn't yet realize how unwise it is to play with him, to lead him on.

"It's toasty in here," he says, patting the bed again, as though she were a dog getting ready to jump.

"I should go home," she says, "I really should." She says this rhetorically, without meaning it, as a way of dignifying her desire for him. She is imagining herself as a container ready to be filled with warm milk, and Howard Rose is the spigot. That's what he makes her feel like: milky. They have been in bed together only once before and already she is obsessed with him. When she goes into Barnes & Noble to study the racks of new books during lunchtime—novel after novel, lined up in their shiny jackets, whoever will read them all?—she is really thinking of him, repositioning herself in the erotic movie that's been running in her head ever since they met.

She gets undressed slowly, self-consciously, undoing her bra (underwire, 36D) to reveal her breasts and then getting into bed with her virginal underpants (plain white cotton, not at all the knock-'em-dead, tiny bits of lacy lingerie her friend Celia sports) still on. He pulls them down over her hips, watching her all the while. When she is stark naked he kneels and parts her legs carefully. He puts his mouth on her nipples, sucking one, then the other. She moves downward, takes his penis in her mouth, one hand circling its base, and runs her tongue round and round the smooth slippery tip, then slowly up and down. She is trying for a hooker's expertise, a kind of erotic multitasking, calling on the wisdom from the issues of *Cosmo* she reads while waiting in the doctor's office or at the nail salon for her nails to dry: "5 Ways to Drive Him Crazy in Bed," or "The 3 Sexual Fantasies He Won't Admit To," or "The 4 Love Spots Every Man Wants You to Touch." She moves back to stroke something she'd read about called the perineum, although she remains vague as to its precise location.

Everyone knew about performance anxiety in men, Judith had always thought, the way they were required to strut their stuff, over and over again, while women had the option of remaining passive in bed, making grocery lists in their head or conjuring up Brad Pitt. She supposed this was why women were taught to coddle the poor, provisional male ego, always on the verge of wilting, why they were taught to gush about how big a perfectly ordinary penis was. What hadn't been sufficiently recognized, if you asked her, was that it was possible for women to be aflutter with their own version of performance anxiety.

She closes her eyes when he moves down her body, preparing herself for the sensation, a mixture of pleasure and a touch of shame, at the flicker of his tongue inside her.

"Do I own you now?" he says into the silence, something he hadn't said the first time they went to bed.

The truth is, she secretly wants to be owned, her independent-woman demeanor notwithstanding: wants someone to take over inside her head and make her decisions for her, leaving her nothing to do but to follow the man holding up the sign saying PLEASURE THIS WAY. How did he know that was what she wanted? And is it the men who know such things who are the real danger to women like her? His penis inside her feels like the missing piece, expressly designed to fill the chink in her armor; she wants to keep it for protection. The question is: Whose protection? Hers or his?

II

SHE KNOWS HIS NUMBER by heart within minutes of his telling it to her, almost instinctively. She writes it down in a mahogany leather address book that she subsequently lost when her bag was stolen while she ate lunch in a coffee shop with a friend somewhere in the city. She would later wonder how much of her life got misplaced in that roomy Coach bag; she dates a lot from the theft of that bag, perhaps wrongly. Her friend's bag wasn't taken, only hers, and for a brief while she seriously entertained the thought that her friend, Celia, was in cahoots with the two hefty girls who were spotted running out of the restaurant. She is suspicious by nature, she hasn't had much reason not to be, although she imagines it would be pleasant to go through the world giving people the benefit of the doubt.

Even at the time—way before it would be clear what he was up to, what she was up to with him—she enters his home number secretively, as though there were something illicit about it. She scribbles it in pencil in her datebook, under his initials,

"H.R." His work number she never writes down, and she will eventually forget it. It's a habit that endures, this abbreviated referral system, as though she were a character in a spy novel, her every action observed by trench-coated men hiding behind newspapers: she uses initials instead of names for the people who mean the most to her, hoping to fool the fates by not spelling things out.

What she means is the same thing she meant when she was eight years old and made pacts with God; she would do this for him if in return he would do that for her. She means to ensure that fate will not, one day, take her unpleasantly by surprise, make her look silly or pathetic in front of knowledgeable witnesses— people who can point to an entry in a diary or phone book and say: *Look whom she loved, how much he meant to her, his name is right here.* She means to ensure that those entries, known by their initials, will become like characters in the posthumous novel of her life: tantalizing biographical clues that only she, the protagonist, could have deciphered and without whose help the puzzle of her life will remain forever unsolved, the outcome forever elusive . . .

"H.R.," for Howard Rose. The name always struck her as off, wrong somehow, as if from another era: it didn't sound like him, and he in turn didn't look like the name. What "Howard Rose" conjured up to her was a vaguely fat, very white-skinned man, someone who maintained strong family ties, who still visited his aging parents in Brooklyn once a week. The real Howard Rose, on the other hand, had been thin, with well-muscled legs. One of the things she found most attractive about him was the way his skin always held a bit of a tan way after the summer. Only deep into the winter would his color fade, turning sallow—that slightly yellowish tone of olive—rather than pale.

As for his parents, she had never met them and he talked about them almost not at all, as though they were best left behind. He dated his life from adulthood: this kind of expeditiousness was new to her. It surprised her to no end that you could organize your life around the locus of the present instead of the past, that you could treat your childhood—and all that went with it, including parents—with so little emotion, as something that was done with.

Several years after their relationship is over, she wakes up from a dream, one of those basic Freudian dreams where she is frantically opening doors in her apartment trying to find the way out. Only it is no longer her apartment but a revised version: extra rooms have been added to it, rooms filled with boxes, and there are large fake-suede pillows on the couch in the living room, the sort of pillows she would never own but that Howard Rose had owned. It is quarter to four in the morning. Outside her window there is the rumble of the city, but inside her apartment it is very quiet, just the faint rustle of her sheets as she turns in bed.

There is no one she can call at this hour of the night and say, "Hi, I'm up," not even Celia. She has spent a lot of time talking with other women about themselves—their bodies, their hair, their mothers, their dashed romantic hopes, everything you could want to know about a person and then some—and still there is no one to call. She is struck by this reality every time she wakes up in the still of the night. She supposes this basic, inalterably lonely fact is why people live with other people, why they eventually get married: it had to be for the simple sustenance of it, a warm body in the middle of the night to curl your own unmoored, woken-up self around, flesh to living flesh, against the quiet and the darkness and the anxieties ignited by one's dreams.

She gets up and pads on bare feet to the bathroom to get herself a glass of water. Somehow she finds it soothing to run herself a glass of water when she wakes up like this—as though the answer to whatever terrors assail her now, a grown woman living on her own, lies somewhere in the primitive rituals of childhood, her mother bringing her a glass of warm milk, however impatiently, when she couldn't fall asleep. When she gets back in bed, she turns on the light for a second, and then she turns it back off. Her room is still there, looking its usual disheveled state, and her dream has been just that—a dream: it is this she wanted to check on, to make sure of. She is the sort of person who is easily disoriented, who has never figured out how to go "left" instead of "right" in an unfamiliar place without mentally playing it out with her hands.

The clock radio near her bed glows the hour in luminous green numerals. It is very dark in her bedroom, but if she strains she can make out shadows within shadows, the outline of her closet door. Inside her closet are her clothes: she dresses with an erratic sense of commitment to fashion, sometimes pulling off a chic, urban look, and sometimes not. She has many black sweaters, in cotton, wool, and two cashmeres, but there is no conceivable way she could patch the various garments she has bought over the past five years—in an array of sizes and styles, depending on her weight and her vision of herself at the time—into a coherent whole, a semblance of a working woman's wardrobe.

She knows that there are women like her mother, whose closets are stunningly organized, with places for bags and shoes, hats and belts, winter and summer wear. She is convinced that if she were capable of maintaining such a closet, her life would be different: she would think coordinated thoughts, never arrive breathlessly late for appointments with florid excuses at the ready, and exercise impeccable judgment in her choice of men. Her bad taste in men was like an instinct gone awry—some effort to get her parents to love her, she supposed, but done ass-backward. It was something she had discussed endlessly with her therapist, Dr. Munch. If only he had stayed around to lead her out of the thickets.

Howard Rose had liked her in tight pants. He liked to look at her in close-fitting jeans, his arms folded behind his head, and imagine to himself what she would look like with her pants off. He told her this early on, how he envisioned her tight, high butt, the roundness of it, silky to the touch, and it excited her to hear herself described this way, like a part instead of a whole. (There was a term for this that she had learned in graduate school, "metonymy," using a phrase to conjure up something larger, but she had never expected to have it applied to herself.) The only time she owned shoes with really high heels—"fuck-me shoes," as

Celia called them—was when she was involved with him; he liked what they did to the shape of her legs.

She returns to him in her dreams in spite of herself, like a dog who's been out wandering but sniffs his way home. She is in fact trying to make up her mind whether to marry another man. His name is Richard and he cares about her in a more respectful, less exclusionary way, one that she has gradually trained herself to think of as love, the sort of love that stays in its place, providing an anchor. Tomorrow she is going to dinner with Richard's parents, signifying the seriousness of their involvement, although a part of her feels a sense of loss at the prospect of signing on for a life with him. For there is still this: seven digits, Howard Rose's number, crumbs of bread dropped along the path through the woods in a fairy tale that happened to be the honest-to-goodness story of her life.

III

BEFORE HOWARD ROSE, she hadn't loved many men—one
or two, at the most, ambivalently. Then again she hadn't been
in the habit of seeing herself as a sexual creature, despite her
looks, someone whose presence stirred men. She wasn't like
her sister, Rebecca, who twirled her hair and spun men around
until they were breathless. Then, too, her amorous history was
a bit shaky; she had a habit of charming men on the first date
only to turn on them on the second. From her teens on she had
been practicing an I'll-reject-you-before-you-reject-me maneu-
ver, fine-tuning her defenses, and for a while it had looked as
though no one would have the patience to break through this
elaborate barricade.

She had lost her virginity at the creaky age of twenty-four,
dishearteningly late by the eased-up standards of her generation. First came several false tries, once with a chatty graduate
student in literature who talked his way out of consummating
the act, and another time with a short but overly virile Israeli

who strutted around naked, brandishing his penis like a proud five-year-old before she had even taken her clothes off. She had been secretly afraid of the aggression, not to mention the pain, involved in intercourse, a reality she had glommed on to in the cautionary, anxiety-producing exhortations of her high school hygiene course while everyone else snickered. Not to mention her beloved Rabbi Klein at Jewish after-school, who rhapsodized about the value of waiting to consummate—"consecrate," he had called it—a relationship until after marriage. She might as well have been living in the 1950s, in a Smith College dorm room alongside Sylvia Plath, meting out kisses, planning to go so far and no further with polite boys from Amherst.

It had finally happened on a June night with someone she had been seeing and found lacking in sophistication but who had appealed to her with an ever-greater luster after the fact, when he had moved on. Ron Zelder was a studious third-year medical student from New Jersey whose hair was beginning to fray at the top. She had been at her thinnest ever—118 elfin pounds and 5'6" tall—when she met him, and for two months he had been infatuated, tirelessly putting up bookcases and cleaning windows in her dark little apartment all the way over on the East Seventies. They had slept together with great zeal, once they had gotten the issue of her still-intact hymen out of the way. But she had eventually scared him off with a barrage of criticisms—beginning with his straight-arrow friends and moving on from there to what she described as his inextricable suburban-ness.

Whatever she had meant by that. Now the suburbs looked good to her, having gotten ever closer to the decisive, much-dreaded benchmark of her thirtieth birthday (hadn't her be-loved Dr. Munch lived in the suburbs?) and still stuck in that same dark little apartment. There was something reassuringly traditional about a man who liked to guzzle beer and watch football with his cronies. On their second-to-last date she had told Ron Zelder that he lacked taste, that his mustard-beige bathing trunks were the color an old man might wear. They had been arguing in his car, over the radio, on the way home from the beach. On their last date he had told her, his voice heavy with finality, that she should find someone more worthy of her high standards. That had been five years ago, and from what she understood he had gone on to marry a blonde anchorwoman from a minor-league TV station.

Maybe she had mistaken the round of suburban life, with its station wagons and family rooms, for something more dull and confining than it was. Maybe Ron Zelder's instincts had been too wholesome for her, too lacking in edge. It was becoming clear to her that she liked a serrated emotional style in men; it seemed that without it she felt she might flounder, or its opposite—feel confined, lose her bearing in vast acreages of tenderness. But look where all her fear of—of what? commitment? convention-ality? boredom? men?—had left her: alone, in a small apartment with an infinitesimal kitchen; alone, at a desk in an office with-out a view other than the building across from her; alone, shop-ping for Mott's prune juice for her infernal constipation late at night at the bodega around the corner. Ron Zelder was probably an eminent heart surgeon by now, with a proud wife whom he whisked off to the Caribbean for expensive winter vacations.

The other man she had loved didn't count because he happened to be her therapist, and by the time she had mustered up the courage to express her love for Dr. Munch he was dying. She had been a contentious patient, often coming late to her sessions, always agitating for more, always looking for flaws in the treatment—slippage from his unconscious. The whole profession got on her nerves, really, these people who set themselves up to heal; failing that, they tried to redirect your personality, tried to get you to accept your *un*healed self.

What she wanted from sessions with a therapist was the same thing she wanted from everything, the animate and the inanimate, from people as well as food, from the movies she went to see and the music she listened to. She wanted a voiding of her own troubled consciousness, a state of permanent satisfaction to replace her own permanent state of unease. She was looking for a rush—the sort of rush other people might use drugs or alcohol for—that went on and on and would make her feel good forever and ever. She wanted her therapist to love her above all his other patients, above his wife and children. (She knew he had a wife and children because it was part of his preferred therapeutic style to impart the occasional personal detail.) Only then would she consider her money well spent. True, Dr. Munch did call her, with gratifying informality, by her first name: this seemed like a step in the right direction. But it was such a tiny one, considering, and in return she leaped forward, she loved him.

It sometimes seemed to her that she had loved Dr. Munch as much as she had only because he paid such close attention to her innermost being. Because her own father was resolutely uninterested in her feelings, she thought of all men as genet-ically disinclined to hearing intimate confidences. Now here was Dr. Munch, sitting with one leg bent over the other, pulling at his earlobe, joining with her in close scrutiny—why she hadn't said such and such to so-and-so, why she had admired Y and hated X, why she still felt bad about not having been chosen as a cheerleader when she had tried out for the squad, why why why she was the way she was. All this time spent by him on the examination of her very own personality, her cloudy mo-tives and ancient conflicts, what had happened to her long ago in some playground—it could make you delirious with love.

But then, as if freshly stumbled upon every time, she would be brought up short by the realization that she was paying out money to the tune of over two dollars a minute for all this dili-gence on her own behalf! It seemed that, short of her killing herself and being reborn as the doted-upon darling of a differ-ent pair of parents, no one would focus on her this way for free. There lay the crux of her disappointment, her overwhelming wish to alert Dr. Munch to his particular shortcomings, her readiness to point out the limits of his chosen profession.

"If you really cared about helping me," she would say, "you'd see me for free."

"I'd like to," he'd answer, leaning back in his big, creaky chair. "But I do this for a living. If I didn't have to make a living, believe me, I would listen to you for free."

"And all your other patients, too?"

"Ah, ah, here we go, being the jealous sibling again. No, just you. Everyone else would have to pay up as usual."

"You're making fun of me," she'd say, but there had been something strangely comforting to her about these preordained arguments of theirs. It was like playing hide-and-seek in childhood, dashing off to crouch behind a tree and then peeking out to check if everyone was still around: she felt recognized by Dr. Munch, felt that he saw her as she was and that she could trust him with the bad as well as the good about herself. Who else, when it came down to it, could you do this with? Your parents, if you were lucky, but her mother had always been a tricky character, someone you couldn't count on to catch you when you fell, and her father was no more available to her as an adult than he had been when she was growing up.

But even as she felt gratitude tugging at her heartstrings she remembered who she was and where she was, and that at the end of the month she would be handed a bill for services rendered. So she remained set on catching Dr. Munch out, proving him unworthy of her attachment. His full name was Selwyn Munch, a name that seemed to her impossibly ornate for a man of such down-to-earth inclinations and suggested to her a questionable grandiosity on the part of his parents (leading her in turn to wonder about the nature of *his* childhood, and why he had chosen to become a shrink).

Sometimes she would comment on the inadequate decor of his office, hoping to wound his pride or at least his aesthetic sense. His office was noncommittal, furnished with strenuously neutral touches that struck her as being all the more acutely revealing. She attacked anything at hand: "I see you like red," she told him accusingly, because he happened to have a small red rug under his chair. "It's my least favorite color." On his walls hung a number of carefully framed photographs of mountains and forest scenes. They looked very professional, as though they might be found in the kind of magazine that was given to dispassionate overviews of the world, such as *National Geographic* or *Smithsonian*. She was quite sure he had taken the photographs himself; she could just see him trudging up a perilously narrow footpath with a clunky camera slung over his chest. She told Dr. Munch that she found the photographs boring. He opened his eyes wide when she attacked his photographs, but that was all.

In the end, of course, Dr. Munch had been as unrequited a love as it was possible to have. He died on her suddenly, without due warning. He died before she had had a chance to straighten everything out, to admit that the fights were just a detour, a way of throwing him off the scent; before she could tell him that she loved him. It had been a recurrence of a long illness that he had failed—or not wanted—to tell her about. Later she would think that this withheld information (information without which she was unprepared for what was to come, until one day she found herself bereft of his attentive presence) had put the whole enterprise of their relationship in jeopardy.

What happened was this: He had gone on an unscheduled vacation—it was spring rather than summer, that proverbial shrinkless August—and he had been curiously, even suspiciously, specific about the details. First he was planning to visit an ailing uncle, and then he was joining his family for one of their athletic trips—featuring canoes and tents instead of hotel rooms—across some carefully selected part of the American wilderness. They had scheduled an extra session that last week. She had been fighting with him more than was usual even for her, and was feeling anxious about his departure. Was he trying to punish her, she wanted to know. "Of course not." He had laughed. "I like our fights, at least most of the time. No, I'm afraid you're stuck with me."

But, as it turned out, she had not been stuck with him, nor he with her. A day before he was due back she received a phone call from a woman who introduced herself as a colleague of Dr. Munch's and curtly told her that he wouldn't be coming back from his "vacation." When she had asked what was wrong, the woman became evasive and suggested she come in to talk. She made an appointment for the next day, which wasn't soon enough; she was filled with panic, which she tried to cover up in the presence of this abrupt, overweight woman with an unbecoming hairdo—an analyst herself, with the diplomas and seating arrangement to prove it—who seemed intent on keeping Dr. Munch's whereabouts and general condition a secret.

It was the most hideous of possible scenarios, Kafkaesque really. She found herself sitting in a strange doctor's office asking the same questions over and over again, as though persistence would yield answers. No, he wasn't dead, it seemed, but he was sick, too sick to plan on seeing her again even if he did get well. What about his other patients, she wanted to know. They had apparently all been told by him before he left on vacation. Why, she wondered, hadn't she been told? And what was wrong with him exactly? Nothing, it appeared, could be divulged. All she was to know was that he wouldn't be coming back and that it was important she find herself another doctor. "I can give you some names," she was told. "There are other good people who can help you." Names! She supposed the doctor had her own chubby, unsympathetic self in mind. She didn't want names! "I want Dr. Munch back," she said, and started to cry. "I'm sorry," the doctor said, her voice losing a little of its edge.

She went home and wrote Dr. Munch a long letter as he lay dying, for that was clearly what he was doing. In it she expressed all the gratitude and love she had failed—not dared—to tell him about while he was dauntingly alive in his office. She wrote him: "I am so sad my tears could fill your swimming pool." She was alluding to a long-standing joke between them—about his needing the money she so reluctantly paid him so he could re-plaster the bottom of his swimming pool. Now she wanted him to know that not only had she not minded paying but that she wished he could, right now, be swimming endless laps across what she hoped was a state-of-the-art pool.

She read the obituaries every day without fail after she heard he wasn't coming back from a vacation he had obviously made up to cover a hideously final absence. There had been a whole network of lies, from the made-up story of the visit to the uncle on. She looked back and marveled at her ability to not see what had been clearly going on in front of her eyes: his skin had been burned by the radiation treatment, a burn she had mistaken for a suntan, and his hair had fallen out, requiring that he wear what in hindsight had obviously been a wig, although at the time she had mistaken it for a strange new Prince Valiant hairstyle. How could she have been so obtuse? She felt herself blush when she thought of it and blamed herself doubly in retrospect for continuing to be difficult, coming late for sessions and arguing about fees, even as Dr. Munch was fighting off a fatal disease.

You could get in terrible trouble not being able to figure out who was on your side. But then she had always been in the habit of cozying up to the wrong people and keeping the right ones at bay; that was one of the things she had hoped to fix in therapy. It went all the way back to fifth grade, when she convinced herself that Kenny Finkelstein really had a crush on her underneath his mean jokes; she kept trying to impress him with ever-more sophisticated vocabulary until one day she understood, from a cluster of girls who were giggling around the sinks in the dank bathroom on the fourth floor, that he truly thought she was weird, irredeemably out to lunch. And undoubtedly this tendency to misread emotional signals went further back to a time before Kenny Finkelstein, to herself in a cradle gurgling up at an inhospitable mother, hoping to win a bottle with all the infantile charm she could muster.

She finally came upon what she was dreading one morning early in May, his obituary in *The New York Times*; it was rather anonymous-sounding if you weren't familiar with him. It made her wonder whether all deaths came down to this, a private affair of grief and memory, impossible to translate. *My Dr. Munch is dead*, she thought, as though she were a child and he were hers alone. Her Dr. Munch, his last bill still unpaid, was gone forever. She felt sadness tearing at her heart, and fury, too. How could he have abandoned her? Had her fighting worn him down—weakened as he was by disease—even further? Was that why he hadn't told her the truth?

Most important: What was she supposed to do without him? At work she closed the door of her office and sat staring out the window, tears streaming down. Less than a month later, three weeks it must have been, she met Howard Rose.

DIGRESSION #1

PEEKABOO, I SEE YOU, out there in the world holding this
book. What's the weather like where you are? It's raining as I
write this, a particularly bleak day in April, *Wuthering Heights*
sort of weather; the bare branches on the tree outside my window are swaying downward in the wind. You're probably female
rather than male, if the statistics about novel readers are right. A
friend of mine, a writer herself, recently diagnosed with cancer
and given to a particularly English style of mordant despair, said
to me only this afternoon: "It may be too late for the novel . . ."
She meant the novel in the traditional sense, orotund and slow,
as told by someone like Thomas Mann.

It may be too late for the novel . . . Here I am, spinning you
a tale in this, the twilight hour for all sorts of classical pleasures,
this age of the global village, of news transmitted via satellite,
of Facebook and e-books . . .

And certainly I'm not a novelist in the Emily Brontë sort
of sense, although I suppose Howard Rose could be said to be

a Heathcliff of sorts. I suppose, too, it could be said that Judith Stone recognizes Howard Rose almost instantly for what he is—a negative romantic hero, a man who deeply dislikes and fears the women he desires. Right from the start, in other words, she recognizes that Howard Rose comes with an "afterwards," that she won't be walking off into the sunset with him. He is the enemy, an enemy with a golden touch and an arsenal of tricks, and her Dr. Munch is dead. There is no one to point her away from the wrong exit, especially when she's been looking so long and she's always had difficulty telling the signs apart: SLOW DOWN. SPEED UP. ENTER. EXIT AHEAD.

The thing about negative romantic heroes is that they exert so much pull on the redemptive scenario lurking within so many women. Save Heathcliff, save yourself. She, for instance, even as he was doing damage to her, imagined that she might save Howard Rose, find the lost little boy inside the hardened adult shell. An illusion, of course, but she has so few, and it's impossible to live without any. Then again, perhaps Heathcliff wasn't glamorous, either. Take away Laurence Olivier playing him and what you have is a man suffering from a character disorder. And character disorders, as you may or may not have reason to know, aren't glamorous. Except in Emily Brontë's time they didn't yet have Freud, and, in any case, people are always larger than the sum of their pathologies.

Peekaboo, let's play hide-and-seek, do you see me, too, you out there, my eyes blinking behind the trelliswork of my fingers? I've covered my face with my hands, covered myself with she, but by now you may be getting impatient with this "she" business and no doubt are beginning to form a picture of her in your mind: a woman who owns some black sweaters and . . . and what? What do you think she looks like, this woman who jousts with her therapist? Does she have any hobbies? Does she bite her nails? Shave her legs every week? Every day? Never? And what exactly is the purpose of this Dr. Munch interlude?

I realize that I should know the answers. But I don't, at least not in any way except the most tentative. In fact, I'm not sure it's possible to write any sort of novel anymore, if you're not supremely canny about literature. Any sort of serious novel, that is, the kind of book that one reads for clues to life. I'm not looking to write a fat escapist tale set on Rodeo Drive that you can butter yourself up in at the beach. I'm not sure, in all honesty, if I *could* do it, but in any case that's not what I want to do right now. I want you with me, figuring out this story along with me: it's the self-conscious postmodernist way, and I don't want to be left behind, do you?

For, of course, you, too, understand that even the truth is mostly provisional, a means of believing in what we believe. There are undeniable truths, of course, but they are mostly small, dull odes to facticity, the truths that come embalmed in concrete, unemotional details that begin and end with themselves: the "truth" of your phone bill; the "truth" of the dry cleaner's being closed after six o'clock.

But even as I write this I realize I am leaving out what is most crucial—the large, vivid truths: the truth of being fired from your job, say; of your husband leaving you; of going into labor. There is no way of undoing these sorts of truths, except in dreams, where you are back in your office, down a long hall filled with other offices; in dreams, where your husband is back on a sunstruck street, looking unaccountably younger, saying something admiring to you about your eyes; in dreams where you find yourself as you were before, your belly not yet distended, the contractions of labor not yet started with their strident pain, the possibility of childbirth as remote as going to live in a Tibetan monastery.

The truth is this: other people are nothing like "truths." So, yes, she is me, but she may also be you, give or take an accident of birth, a few kind or unkind strokes of fate.

I will tell you this: Although her name is Judith Stone, her paternal grandfather wouldn't have recognized his last name in this version—an easy-to-grasp diminution of his own weightier, more ethnic-sounding surname. The first name, Judith, suggests in turn an undoing of the homogenization of Stone: it is her father's concession to his roots, a glance backward, a nod at his tribal context—fraught with an inexplicably dark history, the history of being Jews in the first half of the twentieth century caught in a Europe intent on blood. He has escaped by virtue of his parents' flight from their native Poland, enabling him to step into the clear, unencumbered light of an American present.

Judith Stone was once a little girl with dimpled elbows and small, high-arched feet; long before she loved Howard Rose she loved to eat grapes and play with dolls. When she was taken on a rare outing with her sister to see *The Sound of Music* she fell hopelessly for Julie Andrews as Maria, shepherding the seven motherless children like a herd of lost lambs, whipping them up matching outfits from the curtains in her room. She developed an even more intense crush on Christopher Plummer's Captain von Trapp. It had to do, I suspect, with the reluctant way he fell for Maria, the flicker of severity that informed his distracted affection for his children. The unexpected, elusive warmth of Christopher Plummer's crooked smile: gone before you know it. It's always the same story, isn't it, the same woebegone version of love we drag around after us, like a toy bunny rabbit with one glass eye missing and the stuffing coming out, and yet he is everything to us.

You can catch glimpses of the child that she was on the home movies that are stored on cumbersome, old-fashioned reels somewhere in the basement of her parents' house. If you looked her parents up in the phone book, were so bold as to imagine them outside the confines of this story, they might reward your interest by playing you the brief, on-screen version of Judith's early childhood. Judith's mother was once fairly adept with the camera; she'd enjoyed threading the film through the projector and onto the spools, then flicking the switch on in the darkened living room. See Judith run down the block in her pajamas; see her splash in the pool, wearing a big grin. And so on.

I wonder: Would you find anything hidden in those home movies—the whiteness of little Judith's legs pumping up and down on a tricycle in her red Keds, the way she smiles at someone off-camera—to explain anything that would come later with Howard Rose? Why she loves reading or why she is always looking to escape her own consciousness? Think, for instance, of the movie *Blow-Up* (one of Judith's favorites). She saw it on a wintry Sunday afternoon with her sister, Rebecca, the two of them transfixed by the film's easy sexuality, by Vanessa Redgrave with her beautiful swinging hair and bared breasts, and by the way in which the jazzy British photographer played by David Hemmings studies an ever-more-magnified image the better to try to understand a murder he has—or hasn't—witnessed. Murders should be relatively easy to prove, all that telltale blood, and yet look how hard it is to establish their uncontested truth. How much harder, then—impossible, really—it is to establish psychological truths. In the end we become who we are on unprovable grounds, in spite of the fact that we might have become otherwise. Truth has little to do with it.

The Judith Stone of back then is grown up now; her breasts are large and her hips are narrow. Howard Rose likes to watch her mince on high heels, as though she were a breathy, openly sexy creature—a *Playboy* centerfold, perhaps, or Marilyn Monroe. She likes to arouse Howard Rose; his penis when erect is smooth and poised as a club. I think she shaves her legs often, but when I get done with this paragraph it could turn out that the woman in this unfinished book wasn't who I was thinking of at all. It's like trying to figure out how your life will turn out before it's actually turned out: if you could do that, you could step in the way of fate, think of yourself and all the people in your life as fictional characters known only by their initials.

But enough of this. You wanted a novel, not a philosophy course, right? A writer's responsibility is to write, even if there's no one left to read, much less impress. A critic in her eighties, known for her formidable opinions, once said to me that it's impossible to write without having someone out there to impress. It struck me as true the instant she said it. Like when you're a kid showing off on a bicycle: What fun is it if there's no one to notice the deft way you turn the corner and spin the wheels, to *ooh* and *aah* at the sheer bravado of it? I trust—I hope—you are out there, watching me race down the block. But even if you're not, it's time for me to get back up on the seat of this book, which I'm inclined to fall off of. Out with the subtext and on with the text, right? Or, as Gary Gilmore said before he was executed by a firing squad: "Let's do it." So come with me and watch Judith Stone collide with her destiny in the shape of a man named Howard Rose, whose fingers moved inside of her with great cunning, making her forget, however briefly, who she was.

IV

SATURDAY MORNING of the day of the night of the party where she will meet her romantic future in the form of a lanky man with a closely cropped beard and dark, liquid eyes, the telephone rings, cutting into Judith's second round of dreams. She has gotten up once already this morning. At nine o'clock she woke with a start, worried that she'd be late for work, but then she remembered it was the weekend, with two whole days stretching ahead of her (how, she often wondered, did they ever catch their bearings in a country like Israel with an abbreviated weekend?), and she snuggled back under the covers to sleep some more.

"I woke you." It is a statement—an abashed one—rather than a question.

"No, no, I was awake." Judith hates when she finds she has phoned someone too early or too late, so she is at pains to persuade errant callers that they are in the right. She clears her throat of its sleepy overlay, the vocal fogginess that was a dead giveaway that she had, in fact, been awakened.

"Judith, I'll call you back later, I feel bad."

It was Gerald, a paperback editor at one of the other publishing houses, one of the few people in her industry she found tolerable beyond any but the most perfunctory of occasions.

"Don't be silly. I was just planning to get up. I mean, I *am* up. Is it very late?"

"Almost eleven thirty. But I can call you back. I only called because we had talked about maybe getting together for brunch or something over the weekend."

"Gerald, please. I'm glad you called. I want to see you, I was planning on it. I always oversleep."

There was silence on the other end of the line, which made Judith wonder—not for the first time—how Gerald managed to do as well as he did in his job, given his inordinate diffidence. Conversation with Gerald—even when he hadn't woken her up—tended to include a lot of tooth-pulling. It was touching, really, this lack of assurance; it was partly what drew her to him. (The other thing about him she had responded to from the start was the clinical depression he openly admitted to suffering from. It was odd how, in an age when everyone confessed to everything, when even incest had moved on to the talk shows, few people she knew admitted to depression; it was clearly the last forbidden topic outside of a therapist's office.) Still, the publishing industry was a sociable one, full of bluster and hype, and Gerald Mausner held a fairly important position within it. He was capable of spending half a million dollars on the basis of intuition alone—a sense that a certain book, some novel or true-crime book or biography that he had read months before it actually appeared in hardcover, would do well in paperback. How did he hold his own? It wasn't as though Gerald wasn't smart enough; she didn't for a minute doubt his brains. What she doubted was his personality, his puzzlingly muted reflexes.

"Gerald. Are you there?"

"Yes."

"Good, let's meet. Soon. I can be ready in a half hour."

She had lots of things to do this afternoon—her weekly manicure, and then she had planned a quick search with Celia for something mind-boggling to wear to the party tonight. Judith doesn't want to breathe a mention of any other plans to Gerald for fear he will interpret this as a form of rejection. Sometimes, when she was feeling irritable, she felt tyrannized by Gerald's sensitivities. Of course, he was also sensitive on *her* behalf, which was what made him endearing.

"I've never known you to be ready in half an hour. You really mean half an hour?"

Judith laughs, feeling exposed. Since childhood, every time she meets a new person she hopes to use it as an opportunity to get rid of some of her more prominent character flaws and reinvent herself. But wasn't it the case that all these attributes of personality—voice, handwriting—were supposed to be fixed by a certain age, written in stone, following you for the rest of your life? She fiddled a lot with her handwriting over the years, slanting it one way and then the other, cramping it up or spreading it lavishly across the page. She had been transfixed for a while by the way lefties wrote, their hands curled around the pen or pencil like a baby's fist, covering the writing as it emerged, endowing the whole activity with more intensity than it ordinarily had. Why couldn't you try on a different personality once in a while? The alternative—which was that you were stuck with the "you" you had already proved yourself to be, forever, down the span of a lifetime—had always struck her as grim. Her habitual lateness, for instance; one of these days she'd stun everyone and show up on time, the new, ever-prompt Judith Stone.

"Forty-five minutes uppermost. I'll hurry. I won't wash my hair." (She calculated quickly that she'd be better off dashing into the shower now and then taking a longer one before the party, when she'd attend to the finer points of female grooming.)

"What are you in the mood for? I'm easy. Or do you want to decide when I see you? I can come get you."

"You're sure it's convenient? We could meet in the middle."

Gerald lives on the other side of town from Judith, way over west, in a tiny apartment that she has never seen but she imagines to be perilously overrun with books. In her mind's eye she sees a bookcase falling on Gerald, killing him instantly, like Leonard Bast in *Howards End*. A female publishing acquaintance who claims to have gone to bed with Gerald before he came out as gay has described the apartment to her in pitiful terms, making it sound like a mousehole stacked with manuscripts and unwashed dishes in the sink, with only a sofa bed in the way of furniture.

"Nah," he says, "that's okay. I could use a walk and it's really nice out today."

"Is it?"

Gerald chuckles at her surprise. Judith's apartment is so

dark and subterranean, there could be a blizzard outside for all she can tell. Added to which, she has never been particularly attuned to the natural world. It seems, for some reason, to take her longer than it does most people to shift from one season to the next, to put away her sweaters and get out her light cotton clothes.

"It's the end of May, Judith. The sun is shining and the birds are singing. A little too cheerful for depressives like us, but not bad. There are crowds of people in Central Park."

"I keep forgetting spring's here. Not that I like the winter. But I hate the summer in New York."

"Just get ready, will ya?" Gerald says, with good-natured impatience. "I'll pick you up in your lobby at twelve thirty."

"I'll be there," she says. "Twelve thirty sharp."

V

IN THE SHOWER, the hot water pelting down, Judith maps out her day. She'd have to book a manicure for three thirty or four o'clock—hope that she'd get one at the last minute with Ivana, who usually managed to squeeze her in—and if she ran out of time to shop for something before the party, she'd probably settle for wearing a black dress, the one with an elegantly severe cut to it. Worse came to worst, there were always her legs to rely on: in spite of a childhood brush with polio that had left one leg a fraction thinner and shorter than the other, she had good legs. (She has never understood how she managed to catch polio, even in its mildest form, after the Salk vaccine was invented; it seemed yet another indication of an unhappily random quality to her life. Where were her parents? Where was God, for that matter? Wasn't anyone watching out for her?) She could have used a bit more definition in the calves, but otherwise her legs were definitely a feature to play up. Maybe she'd stop and buy a dazzling pair of stockings at one of those innumerable stores that had sprung up around the city expressly to carry exquisitely designed hosiery. She liked wearing imported brands, expensive as they were—French or Italian pantyhose, with foreign phrases and currency markings on the package; she figured the Europeans knew what they were doing when it came to the subtleties of undergarments. All those centuries of ruling the world before Americans came along must have given them an edge in something . . .

Stepping out of the shower and reaching for a towel, Judith catches a glimpse of her nude body in the bathroom mirror, flushed a deep pink from the moist heat. The lines of her back—broad and strong, like a peasant's—and the way her neck is set a bit more squatly than she would have liked put her in instant mind of her mother. A pity, she thinks as she brushes her teeth, that you couldn't dictate your genetic endowment ahead of time, perch in the heavens on God's shoulder, a tiny concupiscent mote, and request Audrey Hepburn's neck or Elizabeth Taylor's eyes or Julia Roberts's mouth.

Judith pulls on jeans and a sweatshirt and, in honor of the spring weather so recently described to her by Gerald, decides to forgo socks with her sneakers. The red message light on her answering machine is blinking, which means someone must have called while she was in the shower. Partly because she is getting late, but only partly, she decides not to pick up the message; she has always worked on the theory that delaying things only made them more satisfying when they finally came.

The theory, ill-conceived as it was, had been a long time in the making and went something like this: the longer she waited—the more she managed to suspend her curiosity—the more likely circumstances would favor her. It was like holding your breath underwater as a child, staying submerged until your chest hurt and then finally popping up, all gasping and spluttering: the world simply had to yield before such discipline, such self-control. The message on her answering machine would be a magical surprise, a reward for her ability to defer gratification. Marlon Brando would leave her a drawled invitation, someone would unexpectedly bequeath her a country manor in Ireland, that kind of thing. Conversely, the quicker she jumped to return phone calls or to open an auspicious-looking piece of mail, the less likely the outcome would be a good one. It was, admittedly, a somewhat magical, not to mention masochistic, way of operating, but she relied on it to protect her from disappointment, from excessive pain. Underneath all her stratagems she had always believed in the inevitability of bad endings. She looked at life this way: the pain she knew was better than the pain she didn't know.

Twelve twenty-five. Judith brushes her hair and applies some blush so she won't look too gray. Where should they go for brunch? Gerald was thoroughly indifferent to food, which she had a hard time comprehending, since she was always in the mood to eat. It was one of the things about him that made him seem fundamentally alien, in spite of their blossoming friendship. That and his gayness. She knew you were supposed to accept homosexuality with equanimity if you were a white, educated female living in New York City in the late twentieth century. Everyone she knew acted like it was the most normal thing on earth, and in fact a lot of the men she knew in publishing were either gay or rumored to be gay. She had worked comfortably with several gay authors on their books, so she couldn't say her feeling of otherness had much to do with any kind of aversion. Indeed, from what she could tell, gay men were the cream of the male crop. Some gay men, that is; some gay men were exactly as uptight and un-evolved as straight men, only gay. But the good ones: it went without saying that they seemed to have a stranglehold on creativity, as well as being the most sensitive, the funniest, the least encumbered by awkward baggage where women were concerned.

Except for the undeniable brute fact that they weren't interested in women, sexually speaking. Judith still found it hard to accept that the thought of a woman giving head, for instance, which seemed to be a dominant fantasy of heterosexual men, did nothing for gays. Women were wallflowers—worse than wallflowers, they were invisible—at the homosexual ball. And despite her best efforts, Judith had trouble envisioning Gerald entwined with another male body, engaged in graphic sexual activity. She sometimes wondered uneasily whether she was an unwitting reactionary at heart.

Twelve thirty-two. She switches the light off by the front door. Gerald would be surprised by her promptness, waiting outside, leaning against the wall, wearing his inevitable shades and his many-zippered brown leather jacket.

VI

AFTER AN EXTENDED CONVERSATION about where to go, as though everything depended on finding the perfect venue, they opt for a Greek diner on Amsterdam Avenue. It was a known quantity and thus unlikely to disappoint, the kind of place that dealt in large laminated menus, bunches of plastic flowers, and food that was an adult version of school lunchroom fare. The weekend menus were a touch more aspirational, featuring eggs Benedict and overly sweet cocktails. As soon as a waiter comes over to their red vinyl booth, Judith orders a Bloody Mary; Gerald, true to his abstemious ways, goes for a Diet Coke. Feeling unwilling to deal with her habitual anxiety, which assailed her out of nowhere and made it hard for her to focus on the here and now, Judith finishes off her drink before their dishes arrive and orders another one.

"It's odd," she says, "I don't like celery per se, but I love celery stalks in Bloody Marys."

"I could see that," Gerald says. "They're a different proposition. One is ornamental and one is your basic ingredient in tuna fish salad. Hey, did you see the placement what's-his-name's novel got in the *Book Review*?"

"I did," Judith said. "It annoyed me so much that I couldn't bring myself to read it. That guy has been treated like a genius since his first underwritten faux-Hemingway book. Was it a rave?"

"Mostly. There were a few qualifications about his treatment of female characters and something else negative, I can't remember what, exactly, but on the whole it was full of praise."

"Are you sorry you passed on it?" Judith asks between bites of French toast.

"No, I still don't see it as the sort of novel that will sell. It's more of a critic's darling."

"How are your eggs? Edible?"

Gerald is playing with his order of scrambled eggs rather than eating them, which was typical for him. Still, Judith worried about his lack of appetite, and the fact that he was so thin. The second Bloody Mary had climbed up her spine and made her feel expansive, less concerned with herself.

"They're okay. Do you have plans for tonight?"

"I do, for a change. I'm going to a party. I barely know the person who's giving it but I thought I'd force myself. You know the Woody Allen quote: 'Eighty percent of success is showing up.'"

"I never knew exactly what he was driving at with that line. Does it speak to the importance of timing or of luck? Or both?"

"Probably both," Judith says, trying to decide whether to order a third Bloody Mary to help see her through the day ahead.

"Do you consider yourself lucky?"

"Not especially," Gerald says, puffing furiously on a ciga-
rette. He favored Pall Malls—lots of them.

"Me, either," Judith says gloomily.

After a meandering conversation in which they catch each
other up on the past two weeks over cups of coffee, Gerald
smiles and takes the bill.

"Let's share it," Judith says.

"Next time."

"Wish me luck."

"Luck?"

"Tonight."

"May you meet the man of your dreams," Gerald says.
"Whatever form he might take."

Outside on the corner of Seventy-Sixth Street, they hug
each other goodbye, and Judith feels struck, as she always does,
by Gerald's feathery physical presence, the knobby feel of his
shoulder blades, as if he's not quite sure he wants to plant himself in this world.

"Gerald!" she calls after his departing back.

He turns around.

"Take care of yourself." It was an odd thing to say, as though
he were leaving for parts unknown. She wants to say even more,
she always has trouble parting from friends—what if, unbeknownst to either of them, one of them will die within minutes
of their leaving each other, struck down by a car—but she can't
bring herself to say, melodramatically:

"Don't disappear."

"Your cuticles, they grow like wheat!"

Ivana the manicurist pulls the goosenecked lamp closer and bends over Judith's nails, pushing back the cuticles with a gray pumice-stone stick.

"My nails are terrible," Judith says amiably, happy to be in Ivana's capable hands. She liked being taken care of, in whatever form she could get it, and even though there was a part of Judith that regarded weekly manicures as an indulgence, it was also her concession to keeping up a professional appearance. "They keep splitting off and then I peel them even more. They get shorter every week."

"Keep your other hand in the vater. Your nails need moizture, Miss Judit. All those books you readin' dry them out."

Judith sinks her left hand deeper into the glass bowl of soapy blue water, swishing around the marbles on the bottom. Ranged along either side of Ivana, at identical tables with goosenecked lamps set with identical bowls of blue water, other manicurists are bent over other outstretched hands. Judith often finds herself wondering how they feel, doing such repetitive, underpaid work day after day. Still, she loves the intimate atmosphere of Eva's Nails, its name attested to in neon script, its flow of regular customers in and out, its brightly lit feminine bustle punctuated by unchanging homey details: the plastic bottles of cheap pink hand cream; the collection of indestructible plants—spiders, philodendrons, wandering Jews, and ferns—by the window; the giveaway calendar from some church bazaar hanging on the wall behind the display of polishes, which were arrayed in a dizzying palette of colors, including silver, green, purple, and yellow, to satisfy every taste.

The Eva of Eva's Nails was a good-looking, high-spirited Hungarian whose specialty was tips and wrapping—supplying women with fake, glamorous talons via the use of tiny, harsh-smelling vials of glue and powder. From what Judith has observed this is a painstaking, time-consuming undertaking that requires constant upkeep, but the results were amazing. Two hours and seventy dollars could buy you a set of the most glorious nails, as natural or as drop-dead in appearance as you desired, the sort of nails Barbra Streisand had sported (improbably, seeing as how she was a psychoanalyst) in *The Prince of Tides*.

Rumor had it that Eva was the personal manicurist to several California stars when they were on the East Coast, and Judith could well believe it, since Eva had something of a show-biz manner herself. Ivana, like all the women Eva employed, was distantly related to her—a second or third cousin on Eva's husband's side. She was a somewhat somber woman under her cheerful front, a few years older than the others, and Judith imagined she was sunk in nostalgic longing for her native land. She had no idea whether this was actually the case—it might well not be since Ivana, like the other manicurists, seemed to embrace everything American with great enthusiasm—but it was what she liked to think. She had great empathy for people who were nostalgically inclined.

"So, how goes the verk?" Ivana asks in her heavily accented, erratic English. She deftly brushes apricot-colored oil around the cuticles on Judith's right hand, takes her left hand out of the bowl of water, and settles her right hand into it.

"Fine," Judith says. "There's just too much of it."

It is unclear to her what Ivana actually thinks she does. To a hardworking woman who had come from Hungary with her two small children and no visible prospects, leaving an alcoholic husband behind, book publishing could only seem impenetrable. It was too economically vague, this eternal taking of writers and their agents to long, expense-accounted lunches, this buying and selling of potentially commercial book projects at heated and secretive "auctions." Judith talks to Ivana about celebrities who may or may not be writing books—people who've appeared on the talk shows or in *People* magazine. It sometimes seems to Judith that the weekly issue of *People* is the one true link between her and Ivana's worlds.

"That Arsenio Hall, he sometin', no? That hair he wear! He make me laugh. Not afraid to say vot he thinks. You write book with him?"

"Not yet," Judith says. She is always surprised by Ivana's interests; she wouldn't have picked the bouncy black talk show host as one of them, but you never could tell who might catch her fancy. She would love to be able to bring Ivana someone juicy, some true-blue famous person with whom she had sat around and chatted. Ivana enjoyed hearing the goods on celebrities; it made her face light up.

"Same color as usual?"

"Yup."

"Red for a change? Yah? Very European."

Ivana rummages around her lineup of colors and plucks out a bottle of scarlet polish, which she holds out toward Judith.

"Vot you think?"

Judith tries to imagine herself with blood-colored nails, for Ivana's sake, but she has never liked red nails. They make her think of Yvonne De Carlo on *The Munsters*, of women with too-blonde hair who sat on the beach playing mahjong. It was hard to envision lying in bed, reading a book, in red nails. Feeling as if she is disappointing the manicurist profoundly, she shakes her head.

"Sorry," she says. "One of these days I'll try. But today I'll stick to the usual."

Ivana taps a bottle against the table and then opens it with the help of an extra-wide rubber band she wraps around its neck. She applies a thin coat of pale pink polish, a variant on the sort of subdued shade Judith has been wearing since she started coming for manicures some years back.

"When you gonna go diff-e-rent color? Sometin' glamorous? No big date tonight?"

"A party," Judith says. "I'm going to a party."

"A party? Put on some makeup," Ivana says. She gazes at Judith critically and then leans over and unexpectedly strokes her cheek. "Take time. Put on rouge and mascara. You pretty girl but you make yourself look plain."

Judith is unsure whether to feel touched by the manicurist's motherly concern or offended that she has been taken for an ugly duckling whose nascent beauty only Ivana has glimpsed.

"I'll put on lots of makeup," she says. "You wouldn't recognize me."

"Yah? You kiddin' me."

Ivana seems incredulous that someone she sees week after week, whose taste in nail polish is so intransigently mild, might be capable of such splashy self-transformation.

"I mean it."

"Haf' a good time. I tink of you tonight."

"Thanks, Ivana. See you next week."

On her way out of the salon, Judith overhears Eva describing one of her clients' apartments to a woman who is getting some tips repaired at the front table. "Stunnink, I tell you, just stunnink. All vite marble and bik enough to put a rollink-skater rink in. But she's some natural lady, even though she's so rich. She act just like you and me."

Outside, walking quickly up Columbus Avenue, her bare feet squeaking slightly in her sneakers, Judith muses to herself how people with a great deal of money or celebrity seemed to win points for doing so little, as though more ordinary folk were only waiting for the chance to put aside their envy and fall into complete adulation. It wasn't only Eva laboring over some woman's nails who reacted this way; she had noticed it in people in publishing as well, the way they outdid themselves rhapsodizing about what a nice person some famous writer had turned out to be. Waiting for the light to change, she felt herself shiver. It was late afternoon, almost evening; a chill had crept into the air and, quite suddenly, it no longer felt like spring.

VII

IN THE END, as she knew would happen, dressed and perfumed and accessorized (silver earrings, silver cuff bracelet, and an arts-and-craftsy brooch stuck high near the collar of her dress), she hadn't wanted to go. First came an hour of growing anxiety as she stood in her underwear, debating what to wear. She was always struck at moments like these by how many of her fashion finds were unwearable. There was the period, for instance, that she had invested in the clothes of some Russian dress designer whom no one she knew had heard of other than the saleswoman who eloquently sold them to her. The clothes were in the sort of unselfconscious ethnic colors—purple and turquoise and emerald green—she never wore and they were bedecked with flounces and scalloped hems. She had imagined they made her look tall and exotic, like a greyhound—and maybe they had, in the store. At home they struck her as faintly embarrassing, like leftovers from a tsarist court.

She had finally taken refuge in wearing something black—unimaginative but steadfast—as she always did, something studiously understyled and of indeterminate vintage. Still, it had required way too much effort to get ready, all that climbing into the raspy clutches of pantyhose and the spritzing of perfume and the fussing with hair. She thinks of the countless times she'd emerged red-eyed from the shower and proceeded to follow an inexorable series of steps, first the gel and then the blow-dryer, and then finally a strategic blast or two of hair spray. Pretending to be a professional, some Guy or Pierre or Yves who has apprenticed years of his life to achieving the perfectly tousled effect on behalf of his nervous clients, who want to look, every single one of them, like someone other than themselves.

And then the all-important face. There she was, standing before the mirror, staring at her too-familiar reflection, trying to enhance her essentially unmodifiable features with subtle touches of shadows and blushers and liners. Not again, she wants to say: not again! The presented self floating out the front door, leading the way with false bravado and rouged cheeks.

Judith Stone had a theory about parties, which was that they were a hopeless way of meeting people for someone like herself, who blossomed only in correct atmospheric conditions. The correct conditions in her case were hothouse—one-on-one, otherwise you might miss the point. Short of being show-stoppingly, room-silencingly beautiful, she couldn't figure out who were the women parties were meant for. Party animals, she supposed, except that she didn't really know any. She assumed party animals were a breed unto themselves: snub-nosed blondes from Texas or places north, flirtier than she could ever be, real Daddy's girls, ready at a moment's notice to sit on men's laps or play with their ties.

"Celia," she wails into the phone, standing with her raincoat already on, a Saturday night with the forecast of late showers. "I don't want to go."

"You never do," Celia says authoritatively. "We know that about you. You never want to go anywhere and then you never want to leave once you're there. Hold it a sec, I put some water on for tea."

In the background Judith can hear a kettle whistling, and then Celia clanking around in her kitchen. The sounds suggested great coziness to her, the predictable comforts of home, and she could think of nothing she wanted to do more on this particular evening than to go over to Celia's small but impressively organized apartment and have one of their intense conversations over Chinese or Japanese takeout.

"Okay, I'm all yours," Celia announces. "Now, I know there's nothing to get anxious about. I'm sure you look great."

"I do not. I feel fat. And, Celia, there's something wrong with my hair. I thought this was such a great haircut but I must be doing something wrong. I tried to blow it out into the same shape they did but I can't. Maybe I should go somewhere else for my next cut. Should I just come over and forget the party?"

"Don't be silly," Celia says firmly. "You're going. What'd you decide to wear in the end?"

"The black," Judith says. "It presented the least problems. Are you staying home?"

"Unless a better offer comes along. I've got some client reports to finish. And I might check out a movie. You know the one with Richard Gere that you saw and I never saw, you know, where he lays out all the Armani shirts on the bed."

"*American Gigolo*. You still haven't seen it? It's been on TV twenty million times already. Lauren Hutton looks unbelievable in it, especially her hair, it's the most incredible color. Like caramel. That's the color hair I want."

The thing about Celia's life was that it always sounded better to Judith than her own, no matter what their respective plans were. She had known Celia for years—through her marriage and move to Boston and then her divorce and move back to the city, where she had gotten a degree in social work—and there had always been this perceived (at least on Judith's side) imbalance between them. It had to do, Judith thought, with Celia's not believing in the possibility of salvation—that one fine day some person or thing would come along, in a flurry of wings, to rescue her from her own life. "No one's going to step in and magically make things right," she had said to Judith more than once. "We're beyond that now. It's all up to us."

"Aren't you getting late?" Celia asks.

"No," Judith says, although the party began at eight o'clock and it's nearly nine. She is beginning to sweat in her coat. "I hate arriving at parties too early."

"Go already," Celia says. "Then you can come home and know you've lived to tell the tale."

"What if no one's nice to me? What if I just stand there like a blob and no one talks to me?"

"Judith, everyone has these anxieties. That's why *Glamour* magazine exists."

"What does *Glamour* or any other magazine have to do with this? Besides which, I asked you to come with me."

"Judith, sweetheart, I wasn't invited."

"But I won't know anyone there!"

"You might meet someone. That's the point of parties."

"I don't like most people," Judith says, darkly, wondering as she says it whether she means it or whether she is just protecting herself.

"That's not true," Celia says. "You can talk to anyone. You're just feeling insecure. Leave. Now. Walk out the door. Think of me sitting home alone."

"It sounds nice."

"Judith."

"Bye."

Judith sits on her bed after getting off the phone, wondering whom else she might turn to with her predicament. There's her sister, but they've been on the outs of late. Gerald? He would understand her panic, no doubt, but she feels a little funny airing her social anxieties on a man who is attracted to members of the same sex that she is. And why the hell does she have to tense up like this, anyway? It's just a party, after all, not her wedding. Almost thirty years old and talented at what she did—which most people took to be more exciting than it was—and here she was, chewing on the same stew of anxieties as ever. At moments like these she missed Dr. Munch keenly: almost in spite of herself she had felt more hopeful after her sessions with him. Of course, what she had come to realize was that it was *his* hope he had infused her with; now that he was gone his hope had vanished with him. And after that disastrous visit to his appointed stand-in, she hadn't begun to look for another therapist, didn't know if she wanted to. Could it be that she's gotten worse in the meantime, that her personality has regressed to its pre–Dr. Munch state? She is sitting on her bed, willing herself to leave, when the phone rings.

"Why haven't you left yet? Go! You'll never know what you missed."

It was Celia, faithful cohort, urging her on. Judith didn't understand women who didn't need female friends the way she did, who didn't bask in the glow of confessions aired and confessions received. She didn't know what she'd do without them, how she'd get through life.

"Tell me you love me," Judith says. "That you'll be my friend even if I'm left standing alone at the party."

"I love you. But I won't if you're still there when I call back in five minutes."

On the way to the party the cabdriver compliments her on her perfume, which he tells her is a big compliment coming from him because he smells women and their perfumes all day. "Kind of smoky," he says. "Different." Judith thanks him and when she gets to the address she has scribbled down on a piece of paper—it is a modern, anonymous-looking building—she gives him what is, by her standards, a huge tip.

VIII

TEN MINUTES into the party, having put her trench coat down in the bedroom and said hello to the hostess, Judith wishes she hadn't come. Madonna is singing in her high-pitched, slightly nasal voice and several couples are dancing in the far corner of the room. There is a table set with drinks and another, at right angles to it, set with food: bowls of guacamole and tabbouleh, platters of cheese, strawberries, and brownies. There are candles in amber-colored glasses and soft lamplight and people standing or sitting on couches, talking animatedly to each other. Everyone looks comfortable, as if large groups were their natural milieu. Only Judith, standing before an array of bottles and glasses, deliberating the caloric advantages of club soda versus the soothing but more fattening properties of something alcoholic, is alone and ill at ease.

"The wrong people have money," someone was saying behind her, "it's been that way forever."

Popping a strawberry into her mouth, Judith Stone is struck

by the comment—its mordant implication that there were wrong (and therefore right) people where money was concerned.

"Howard," a woman says admiringly, "you're always so cynical."

"If Howard had more money," someone else is saying, a man, his voice deeper than the first, "he could be a rich Marxist."

They all laugh, and Judith turns toward them with her glass in one hand (she has gone with the wine), pushing her hair back from her forehead with the other (a habitual gesture when she feels tense). She sees two men and a woman. One of the men, whom she puts together with the deeper voice, is short and slightly paunchy, with a pleasant-looking face. The other man—he of the witty remark—is slightly taller and thinner. For some reason she looks down at his feet and notices that he is wearing scuffed shoes, with toes that are unfashionably pointy.

"Hi there," he says. His voice is cool and light, almost boyish.

Judith looks up at his face, which is at odds with his voice. His eyes are dark—wounded-looking, she thinks, like the eyes of an animal at bay—and it isn't that he looks old so much as that he seems inherently unyoung, as if life had pushed him ahead of himself.

"Hi," she says, pushing her hair back again. She wonders whether she is blushing.

"This is Alan," he says, pointing to the other man, "and I'm Howard Rose." He goes on to introduce the woman—it's some short name like Gail or Lynn. Judith isn't paying close attention because she's trying to figure out whether the woman is with him or with the other man. "We're all lawyers."

"Nice to meet you," Judith says, smiling vaguely in their general direction.

"We thought we knew almost everybody here," Alan says. "But we don't know you."

"Oh." She laughs nervously. "I actually don't know a soul. Except the hostess a little bit. I'm Judith."

"I like your earrings," Gail—Lynn?—says, and then: "What do you do?"

"Thanks," Judith says, fingering the embossed silver hoops in her earlobes. She had wondered as she was getting ready whether to go with them or a more obvious pair. "I work in publishing."

Chitchat: she loathed it, considered it unworthy of a genuinely evolved personality. What was the phrase Wordsworth had used? She had studied him in college and hadn't much cottoned to him, except for the one poem, "Intimations of Immortality," and the concluding line: "Thoughts that do often lie too deep for tears." Judith had identified: she often thought of herself as someone who wouldn't be able to stop crying once she got started, although she wasn't sure that's what Wordsworth had meant. Still, could you possibly have deep thoughts and be good at chitchat?

"Marketing?" Alan asks. "I know a couple of people in that end of the business."

"Actually," she says, "I'm a book editor."

"An editor," the woman whose name she's unsure of says. "That sounds interesting. I used to be friendly with someone who was Herman Wouk's editor. Have you worked on any books I would have heard of?"

"You keep doing that," the man named Howard says to Judith, out of the blue, as if they've always been on close terms.

"Doing what?"

"Pushing your hair back like that."

"Howard has always fashioned himself," Alan offers, "an astute observer of women."

"It must be a tic," Judith explains unnecessarily, "one of many in my repertoire."

They all laugh, and Judith finishes off her wine, hoping she isn't blushing like a beet.

"I like it, actually," he says, as the other two watch them.

"I didn't catch your name," Judith says to the woman.

"Gayle," she says. "Spelled importantly, with a 'y' and an 'e.'" She smiles, revealing very white and even teeth.

"Short and sweet," Alan says. "And important, like you."

"I'll have you know I'm of average height," Gayle says, drawing herself up with a feigned sense of injured dignity.

"Yeah, what can you do, Jews are a short race so anyone over five feet qualifies as a giraffe."

Judith laughs appreciatively.

"Alan, darling, I'm hungry," Gayle says, linking her arm in his.

"Time to eat," Alan says. "We'll catch you guys later."

"Nice to meet you," Gayle says. She is wearing a red silk blouse, a life-of-the-party sort of blouse, and a pair of tight-fitting navy wool slacks that show off her small waist and trim body. As she and Alan move away, Judith is conscious of him, the one named Howard, looking first at Gayle's body and then at her.

"Are you happy?" he asks her in his cool, light voice.

"Not really," Judith says, wondering at first whether he has asked her if she's hungry or happy and then wondering if he cares either way or is merely being jarringly intimate.

"Well," he says, "it's just us now."

James Taylor, pining for Carolina, has replaced Madonna; the whole party seems to have quieted down, or maybe she's just imagining it. She's so tense she can feel her jaw tightening.

"Yes," she says, "it seems that way."

"You remind me of someone," he says, scratching at his close-cropped beard. He has a wide, full mouth and clear, olive skin. A slightly vulpine face, probably not to everyone's taste, but to hers. Something about him makes her sad, it must be his eyes; she wants to make him happy. She has a quick image of them holding each other, blocking out the world.

"I liked him," she says. "Your friend, Alan." She thought of the cabdriver telling her he liked her perfume.

"That's funny," he says musingly, as though she has said something infinitely complicated.

"What?"

"I didn't peg you for a nice-guy type of woman."

"Oh, really?" Judith says, injecting a note of annoyance into her voice. "Isn't he your friend?"

What she feels is less annoyed at the presumption of his comment than curious. She has a breathless sense that this man

77

she has just met is about to tell her who she really is, the truth about her, unbeknownst to anyone but him.

"Yeah," he says. "Alan's a pal. Gayle, too. Business associates, you might say. We're all in the same line of work, and Alan and I play squash together sometimes."

"What kind of law do you practice?" she asks.

He stares at her and then mouths an answer, as though they were playing an elaborate and unspecified guessing game.

"I didn't catch it," Judith says.

"Criminal," he says. He cocks his thumb and index finger and pretends to shoot it, like a gun. "Bad guys."

"Bad guys?"

"I defend them."

"Oh," she says, noticing his longish, squared-off fingers—spatulate is what she thinks it's called. She wonders what his hands would feel like on her breasts.

"You look lost in thought," he says. "Where'd you go?"

He seems to be standing on top of her, not missing a thing, attentive to every unspoken flicker of her mind. Perhaps it was a technique he had learned in law school, or maybe it's just his eyes, wandering all over her.

"I was wondering," Judith says, "if what they say about butchers—that they work out their violent feelings by hacking away at cow parts—is true of lawyers."

"How's that?" he asks.

"I mean," she says, "aren't people who become butchers supposed to be sublimated murderers? I wonder if criminal lawyers feel a kinship with criminals that leads them to represent 'bad guys,' as you call them, in court."

"You have an interesting mind," he says. "I'll have to think about it. But first I'm getting myself a drink. How about you?"

"Thanks," she says. "I'd love some more wine."

"Don't," this strange man named Howard says, "move."

The second he heads for the bar she goes to get her coat, which has gotten buried under a pile of coats, at least two of which she mistakes for hers, and without bothering to say goodbye to anyone, under cover of music and conversation, she leaves the party. It isn't like her to be so decisive, or so impolite, but something about this man unsettles her and she can't afford to waste any time. Out in the hallway, waiting by the elevator, she can hear her heart thumping in her chest, as though she's made a daring escape.

IX

THE NEXT DAY, Sunday, about noon, she is reading *The New York Times* in her nightgown (her favorite overwashed flannel, which smells like essence of cotton), scanning the wedding announcements while eating unbuttered whole wheat toast with a smidgen of strawberry jam. She is thinking about calling her sister and offering to take her nephew, Charlie, to the park, in between thinking about the man she met last night at the party, when the phone rings.

"Bitch," he says.

She should've hung up, then and there, shown him—shown herself—that she's not the kind of person to be spoken to that way. If she had, the whole drama would never have unfolded. But she doesn't: there was something exciting to her about male hostility; at least it told you what you were up against.

"Who is this?" She knows who it is, she recognizes his voice the moment she hears it.

"I thought I told you not to move."

He sounds steelier today, less boyish. This must be the voice he uses in court, on uncooperative witnesses: *I thought you said earlier that you were out of town on the day of the alleged crime.*

"I had to go," she says, as though she owes him an explanation.

"I want to see you," he says.

"Why?"

She is flattered by his directness; scared, too. Is he intriguingly different from the more average kind of man, inquiring into her state of happiness within seconds of meeting her, or some kind of disturbing anomaly?

"I find you attractive," he says. "Very attractive."

She is briefly silenced by this head-on admission.

"Hello," he says, as though he were an astronaut attempting contact with another planet, "hello hello."

"Really," she says belatedly.

"It's a combination of things," he says. "Your mind. Your legs. Your tits, what I could make of them."

"I think I find you nuts," she says, but it is a weak gesture, a hand raised against the glare of the sun.

"I've got an idea," he says, undeterred.

"What?"

"I'll pick you up in half an hour."

"I can't," she says. "I absolutely can't."

"Sure you can," he says.

"I've got other plans."

"Dump them."

"No," she says, but she is hoping he won't give up.

"Dinner, then," he says. "Tonight."

"I don't even remember your last name," Judith says. This isn't true, of course, his name had been imprinted on her brain from the moment she heard it, but she wants to impart a degree of casualness on her end that won't give away her interest.

"Rose," he says. "Howard Rose. Criminal defense lawyer and sublimated murderer. Cousin of the lowly butcher."

She laughs, pleased that he has remembered her little theory of the evening before.

"I don't know," she says.

There was something off—irregular—about him that she couldn't quite place, an undercurrent that made her more anxious than usual, that had made her bolt from the party the night before.

"I want," Howard Rose says, his voice gone husky, "to see you. But I'm not going to ask again."

"Okay, okay," she says.

How quickly she could lose him! One more second of resistance and he would be history, her world gone back to its usual contours, no longer swollen with desire.

"Good," he says. "Seven o'clock? I'll pick you up."

What the hell. This man, Howard Rose, definitely struck her as less than optimal news. Sexy, maybe—if you considered sharks sexy. An example of what Dr. Munch would describe as her unerringly bad taste in men, for sure. Then again, she has never been quite sure where the erotic fit in, how it went with the other parts of life. How did fucking, that is, fit in with backyards and wiping your kid's snotty nose and the way your mouth tasted in the morning when you first woke up—"dragon breath," as the mouthwash commercials so indelicately called it? Was marriage the end point of romance and romance the end point of fucking? Or were they all really meant to be in separate compartments? She had come to sex late, after all, and maybe her whole notion of it was skewed, had too much to do with winning over the enemy. Still, there was something vulnerable about this man that she was responding to as well, those tacky shoes, a feeling she had that he spent a lot of time by himself.

"Fine," she says. She must remember to shave her legs. She tended to let them go—her underarms, too—when she wasn't seeing someone.

"See you," he says. And then, softer than a whisper, more like a sigh, he adds: "Bitch."

Is she imagining it or did he actually say it—"bitch," once again, at the end as in the beginning, before he hung up? Which brings her to a more important question: Was Howard Rose appealingly out-of-the-box or just plain, out-and-out crazy? Should she be running for her life instead of reminding herself to shave her legs? She's never gotten the whole relationship thing right, the instinct for self-preservation eluded her. It had to do with the undeniable streak of despair in her character, her sense at the end of most weeks, come Sunday night, that there was something dismal about the prospect of Monday morning.

Then again, looked at in a certain light, life struck her as inexcusably repetitive: just when you got your hair clean, you had to shampoo it all over again. Besides which, she has never quite made up her mind whether this hallowed thing called life was worth preserving herself *for*: too much could go wrong— did go wrong, in fact. She certainly wasn't one of those people who counted their blessings. Far from it, she was in the habit of wondering whether things could get any worse. Well, here was the opportunity to find out. If what was bad for you might kill you, it also, she reasoned, might unexpectedly save you.

DIGRESSION #2

SO, YOU MUST BE THINKING, finally they meet. Here comes Howard Rose, flying through the sleeping village, in his black cape. See Judith Stone, preparing for the party, like Cinderella before the ball. It could be a fairy tale, if it weren't so bogged down in the gunk of reality—the sticky bits of sleep that are stuck in the corners of her eyes when she wakes up next to Howard Rose, the yellow cake of Dial soap that sits on the ledge of his bathtub, encrusted with a few pubic hairs.

The plot, that is, thickens, in spite of my doubts. Which is all to the good. I mean, that's what you wanted, right? Anything else and you would accuse me of writing for myself—masturbating on the page, so to speak. And that's not a criticism I would warm to, except in a flush of embarrassment. Then again, the connection between embarrassment and arousal strikes me as singularly underexplored. I would explore it further right now, meander about in the byways of speculation, except that I want to show some spine—some stick-to-itiveness—and get you back to the story.

But first, try this on for size:

"Arousal is a consequence of excitation. It is an alarm or mobilization signal in the organism. Arousal always affects all the body's organs, particularly those with key survival functions."

What do you make of that? On the face of it, it presents a rather puzzlingly pragmatic approach to sexual excitement, wouldn't you say? Do breasts and vaginas, for instance, qualify as organs with "key survival functions"?

I copied it down some time ago, on one of those Post-it notes. I thought the quote would come in handy, although I can't remember right now where I got it from. By the by, those Post-it pads are useful little gizmos, aren't they? At least as transformative as the cell phone and the fax machine and Federal Express before that, if not more so. In Judith Stone's office they have stacks of them, in all sizes and colors, I know, I've seen them there in the supply closet, under the shelf with paper clips and Scotch tape. Yellow's purportedly the most popular color, which makes sense on the face of it. Metaphysically speaking, yellow doesn't arouse too many associations beyond itself, which is what you want in a professional setting. No arousal as a consequence of excitation. They say pale green has a calming effect—that it's good for hospitals and such—but I don't know. Anyway, I seem to have gotten stuck here, ruminating about Post-it colors like an interior decorator; it must have something to do with the weather today, a dark and rainy day in early December, when all I wanted was to get back to the story.

I am her: but you know that already.

Ah, but what I don't know is this: Who are *you*, you I am wooing with every leap of the imagination I've got? Would you prefer to be reading a biography of Hoover? Herbert or J. Edgar? The chicken-in-every-pot man, or the paranoid, cross-dressing director of the FBI, take your pick. Or maybe it's science fiction you like, tales of intergalactic derring-do?

This writing of fiction, drawing on bits and pieces of reality as fiction inevitably does, is such a deliberate effort, it takes so much tuning-out of ongoing life, that I'd like to know before I go any further whether there's a receptive audience: Can I, for instance, trust you with my characters? Will you watch over them? Even Howard Rose, you've got to care about him in some way, too, or the game's up.

No one's all bad, or so they say. It all comes back to the eye of the beholder, doesn't it, what kind of perspective you take. Horror, in the end, may be only a matter of being too close up for comfort, like a child having a nightmare. Take a few steps back or turn on the light and the monster looming over your bed is just the shadow cast by your coat that you threw over the chair when you came into the room . . . unless, of course, you—like Judith Stone—believe in the possibility of ogres, real-life ones. And that, in turn, depends on your personal history: who your parents were, how they viewed the world. The world begins at home, with you as a cuddly, soft-skinned baby drinking in the psychic milk—the fears and longings, the distrusts and preferences—your mother dispenses along with her more conscious caretaking. (Here is Selma Fraiberg, writing about the evolution of infantile anxiety in *The Magic Years*: "The future mental health of the child does not depend upon the presence or absence of ogres in his fantasy life, or on such fine points as the diets of ogres—perhaps not even on the number and frequency of ogres. *It depends upon the child's solution of the ogre problem.*")

The monstrous, in other words, has its first expression as an internalized sense—and only later on gets its due expression in actual, externalized form. The monstrous need not be loud, for instance, or even violent. (Henry James, to whom Judith devoted a summer's worth of reading when she was in her late teens, wrote almost wholly about the prickling apprehension of just this subtle, now-you-see-it, now-you-don't form of monstrousness.)

So tell me, how well have you solved your ogre problem? Hmm? What are your substitute monsters? Whom do you hate, deep inside, away from the light of day? I keep wondering about you, who you are, who you might be. Maybe I've passed you on Eighty-Sixth Street, getting out of the subway? Or waited behind you in line at a Citibank ATM? I can't pinpoint you, that's for sure, so go ahead, tell me your dirty secrets. I've already told you mine (you don't really believe, do you, that I'm anyone but a writer pretending to invent a character named Judith Stone—anyone, that is, the absurdities of plot notwithstanding, but a woman in love with a man named Howard Rose) and there's more, pages more of dirty secrets, where those came from. Strictly from your perspective, there's nothing to lose: you've got the goods on me. I stand here, red-handed, pressed like a flower (from a bouquet, say, proffered by Howard Rose, wrapped in cheap white paper printed with violets) between the pages of a book, flitting between sentences, offering you myself in all my guises.

X

"OPEN YOUR LEGS," Howard Rose says. "Wider. That's it."

In the dark, under the canopy of sheets, he is an explorer and she is a cave full of lights and textures and squishy sounds.

"Don't be shy," he says. "You're a shy girl, aren't you? Although it would be hard to say just how shy on first acquaintance."

"We've only just met," Judith Stone says, her head on the pillow. His sheets are light blue, the color of expensive men's shirts, and smell faintly of detergent.

He pulls his finger out of her and licks it as she watches, as though she were a dish of ice cream.

"You taste," he says, pausing, "very good."

"Don't all women taste the same?" she asks, genuinely curious but also trying to shift the focus, make a general human principle out of a mortifyingly intimate observation.

"No," he says. "They don't. Some taste too musky."

"That's not very nice," she says, wrinkling her nose.

"Not nice to say or to notice?"

"Either."

"I want to fuck you again," he says, just like that. "But first I want to bend you over a chair so I can admire your tits and ass for a while."

Immediately she sees herself, breasts dangling, rump raised toward the heavens, a show horse ready to be mounted. There's something about the image—its utter facedown passivity—that both alarms and thrills her. Who is this man she has met last night at a party and why does he think he can talk to her this way?

"No," she says. "I can't, really. I've got to go home."

"Stay," he says, "you've got nowhere to go." He unfurls his tongue inside her mouth.

"Howard." She says his name as though she were gasping for air.

"What, kiddo?"

For a moment he sounds like Humphrey Bogart, trying on tenderness for the little lady. He leans back on one elbow, like someone at a picnic resting between courses.

"You barely know me. I'm not like this usually."

"Like what?" His eyes have narrowed, she can't tell whether he's getting bored or angry.

"I don't know," she says. "I mean I'm not some type you pick up at a party."

It isn't the explanation she means to make, but the truth—that she can't separate sex from emotional attachment, fucking

94

from conjurings of love, that she can't stand the thought of not seeing him again and again—is impossible to admit to so early in the game.

"Look," he says abruptly, "no one's forcing you."

"I'm aware of that." She is looking at his body, his penis curled against his thigh, no longer ramrod straight, a piston drilling into her. The volatility of penises still surprised her, the way they went from strength to weakness, erect one minute and drooping the next, like neglected flowers. It was quite a responsibility for women to take on, arousing men. No wonder they were always being told to coddle men's egos: egos translated into penises, of course, and look how susceptible they were.

"Uh, I think I'm gonna take a shower," he says, and leans over to turn on the radio. A woman's voice comes on, crooning about some misbegotten love affair.

"So that's it," she says, half questioningly.

One minute it seemed he couldn't get enough of her, the next he was washing her off like sweat after a day's labor.

"Looks like that, for now, doesn't it?"

She picks up his hand, but it remains inert so she lets it drop.

"This is a little abrupt for me," she says. "I'm not sure what you want me to do."

Was he nuts or what, shifting gears like this? And why were nutty men like him the ones who seemed gifted in bed? Even in her limited experience she had been struck by this apparent disparity: it was as though erotic talent and psychological wholesomeness existed in an inverse ratio to each other . . . She'd have to ask around about this guy. Inquire some more into his background. Something told her now was the time to extricate herself. In fact it couldn't be any clearer, it was a directive coming at her: DANGEROUS CURVE. SLOW DOWN. EXIT AHEAD. Except that she was reading it wrong as usual, confusing one set of signs for another: SPEED UP. ENTER HERE. SMOOTH SAILING AHEAD. If her life were a movie, a scary film directed by someone who had taken lessons from Hitchcock, there'd be a flash-forward now to a woman lying on a bed, her naked thighs streaked with black garters, a trickle of blood running down the sides of her face like tears.

"Poor baby," Howard Rose says, standing in his bathroom door. "My poor lonely baby."

"I'm not lonely," Judith says stiffly, but she doesn't move to get up. Outside there is the sudden blaring of horns beeping at once, then a man yelling obscenities. For a few moments she has forgotten where she is; she might be a castaway on some erotic island, but the street noises bring her back to New York City, to being a woman in a man's bed in a white-brick apartment build-ing on a block with trees and a church.

"Come over here," he says, sitting back down on the bed. "I know what you need."

She puts her head in the crook of his arm. Another song is on the radio now, an old Beatles tune, Paul McCartney's clear choirboy singing of "The Long and Winding Road." She knows so little about Howard Rose or his past: Had he ever loved the Beatles the way she had?

"Your tits," he says, "are amazing, do you know that?"

Her breasts under his hands feel warm and her nipples pop

up as if on cue. He puts his mouth over her right nipple and sucks it ferociously. Why, it was he who was the lonely baby, just a hungry, lonely baby at heart, there was nothing to be afraid of, she should have known.

"I want you," Howard Rose whispers. "I want to fuck you so you forget where we are."

She puts her hand on his penis, which is stiff and hard again. Who was this man? When she had first seen him across the room last night he hadn't even seemed her type; he was thinner than she went for, and she hadn't liked the loping way he moved. There was something larger that was wrong, as well, she could tell by the way he could turn his interest on and off like a light switch. But it was too late to pay attention to the warning signals, for here he was, inside her again, a penis like velvet, and here she was, filled up with him, alone no more.

"I've got you," Howard Rose says, "I've got you now, little Miss Judith."

XI

THE MORNING AFTER the night she has gone to bed with Howard Rose, Judith Stone is standing in a crowded subway car,
one hand gripping the overhead bar, stuffed between people—
strangers, no one she would have picked to stand so close to
this early in the morning—on the way to work. She is lost in
thought, in the midst of one of her usual daydreams, in which
she envisions herself living a different life—the life she was
surely meant to live—far removed from the swelter and clamor
of the Manhattan subway.

In the version of "The Judith Stone Story" that dances before her she has just finished parking her car (although in real
life she has never learned to drive) and is carrying her groceries
across a tree-lined street to a house with a front porch. It is a
small town somewhere in upstate New York—the kind of town
she has passed through on trips and has glimpsed in movies.
But no, better yet, she is living in another state altogether—one
farther north, like Vermont or New Hampshire, rich in foliage

and sky. So, a grocery bag balanced on either hip, the alternate version of Judith Stone walks up the steps of her front porch (replete with a swing and hanging planters), the heroine of a quiet but entirely honorable existence. In this, the life she would have chosen if lives were there for the choosing, her hair is scooped back into a simple yet flattering ponytail, and her face is blandly pretty. She looks, in short, somewhat like a character meant to be played by Sissy Spacek, if Sissy Spacek were an actress meant to play a character like her.

Standing in the subway under the glaring lights, her other hand keeping a firm hold on her shoulder bag, the real Judith Stone, looking nothing like Sissy Spacek, is warming up to this retelling of the story of her life when she is jostled against the small, stony-faced man standing next to her. She's done no more than brush against him, but you can never be too careful in this city, someone might be carrying an artillery's worth of rage waiting to go off at just so casual a cue.

"Excuse me," she says, just in case.

The man nods imperceptibly, and she tries to return to her fantasy: There is a dog, some sort of small, wiry breed (in real life she keeps a cautious distance from all animals, but a dog belongs in her counterlife), who stands inside the screen door, his tail wagging delightedly at the sound of her feet on the stairs. And there is a husband, a husband would be nice to have—a stabilizing ingredient; she quickly sketches in Howard Rose, transforming him into a high school biology teacher with a genial mustache (in real life she doesn't much like mustaches on men, they suggest something enfeebled to her), and is moving on to a homey kitchen with an enameled spice rack . . .

"Cunt," someone whispers, cutting into the smell of her cooling pies filling the homey kitchen (in real life she cooks little and has been known to pass off Duncan Hines chocolate-chip cookie mix as her own). Packed between swaying bodies, Judith looks around, unsure where the voice is coming from and whether its message is being directed at her.

"I make you nice 'n wet," a male voice whispers.

She keeps her eyes fixed high, on the advertisements for dental work and acne cures and treatment for hemorrhoids. Someone on this train is speaking to her like the most brazen of lovers, like Howard Rose, defying all propriety: Who could he be? She thinks it is the same man she has bumped into, but she is afraid to meet his gaze lest she fuel him further. She rummages around in her head, trying to reestablish herself in a rural mode, conjuring up a pair of towheaded twins scrambling around on a play set in a capacious backyard, but she has only one more stop to go and there isn't enough time to make the idyllic images stick. She concentrates instead on the woman sitting opposite her, her legs crossed, reading the *New York Post*. The woman appears to be around her own age, or maybe a little older. She is chewing gum with great intensity, which is something Judith never does in public, and she is wearing clunky running shoes paired with a crisp, ready-for-business suit, a fashion combination that Judith herself has never favored, even if it made sense for commuting.

The train screeches to a stop, and Judith pushes her way out behind a woman with two Macy's shopping bags. The differences between people were unceasing, and amazing in their variation. It was like taking a summer vacation in Odessa, the very prospect boggled the imagination. Were there, Judith wondered, beach chairs in Odessa? Suntan lotion? Did they serve drinks poolside with little straw umbrellas stuck in them? She knew about summer dachas in Odessa from watching the eleven o'clock news; it was where Russian heads of state repaired to when they wanted to relax, rather than the Hamptons or Martha's Vineyard or Maine, but it seemed ungraspable to her all the same, like a resort set in a dream, or in a surrealist foreign movie, a movie by Fellini, filled with an unlikely assortment of clowns, midgets, and fat ladies.

And then, for no reason she can think of, trailing her way behind a ragtag group of people out of Grand Central Station, she finds herself musing on the simple but telltale difference in the matter of losing things. Why was it that some people seemed to go to their graves with all their original possessions intact, while others couldn't hold on to anything? As she waits for the light to change so she can cross Park Avenue, Judith ponders this puzzling discrepancy. Take her grandmother, for instance: every bottle of Chanel No. 5 her grandmother had ever owned had been arrayed, in emptied glassy splendor, on the small, skirted vanity table that stood in the entrance to her bedroom. (Her grandmother's preserving impulse had been perhaps the most interesting thing about her, the way she hung up whatever dress she was wearing the minute she got home so she wouldn't have to tax the material with undue dry cleaning.) Those chunky square perfume bottles had fascinated Judith; she would pick up one or the other whenever she visited and sniff the stopper. In the end, the bottles had outlasted her grandmother, and Judith remembered wondering at the funeral whether someone—her own no-nonsense mother or one of her aunts—had gathered them all up and thrown them away after she died, or whether they had been kept in permanent tribute to her memory.

And why did she, Judith, seem to spend an inordinate part of her waking life looking for things that had been lost or misplaced? At least once a week she found herself on the frantic trail of retrieval for something minor yet essential—a favorite lipstick, a book, a single earring. Was it an inborn difference, like the gene for brown eyes—or like shyness had recently been proved to be—or was it a learned (albeit maladaptive) trait?

On this bright, unseasonably warm morning in June, a little after nine thirty, the city is at full tilt. The traffic roars down Lex, all the cars, buses, and vans in a hurry to beat the next red light. Judith passes a newsstand full of glaring newspaper headlines and shiny magazine covers featuring unreasonably beautiful young women dressed for summer in flimsy bits of clothing and lots of golden skin. *Think tangerine*, advises one magazine; *the new easy wear*, suggests another. She catches sight of these quick, breezy messages on her way by and immediately files them away, as if they might actually have some bearing on the months ahead, as though she, too, will be cavorting in the sand, merry and *sportif*, alongside one of those six-foot, tawny-haired beauties.

Rounding the corner, she sees that the Korean grocery diagonally across from her office building has its usual display of glistening, precisely arranged mounds of fruits and vegetables out front—apples, oranges, cherries, and grapes; cucumbers, tomatoes, eggplants; little Styrofoam trays of cubed grapefruit and melon sealed under plastic wrap. Every day, as if by magic, the same neat piles reappear, a testament to the unceasing exertions of the unsmiling man who runs the store together with an unsmiling assistant. Sometimes in the afternoon she takes a short walk over to the grocery from her office, just to get away, for a coffee or a diet soda. But in the mornings on her way to work she isn't up to either of the men. She feels lazy and inadequate when faced with their swift calculations at the cash register, the guttural-sounding language they hurl at each other, their deft bagging of purchases. *Take it easy*, she wants to say to them. *Let's get to know each other. This is too impersonal for me.* But she doesn't, of course; they'd take her for a crazy person if she did more than smile.

Judith enters the high-ceilinged lobby of her arctically chilled building and walks across the echoing marble past a uniformed attendant toward the bank of elevators at the far end. She pushes the button for the eleventh floor; it lights up responsively at her touch. She is alone in the elevator, so she takes out a mirrored compact and angles it for a quick appraisal. She catches herself in a tiny reflected patch, staring out, her eyes pouchy with fatigue.

"Go-od morning. We're looking bright-eyed today, aren't we," her new executive assistant, Dolores Lawson, singsongs by way of greeting.

Judith, slightly startled by the salutation, pulls up one side of her mouth in the weak semblance of a smile. She hardly knows this gray-haired woman who sits so visibly at the ready outside her office, having hired her last week after Sheryl, her old assistant, gave sudden notice. (The job is, in fact, mostly secretarial in nature, but it seemed no one wanted to be known as a secretary anymore, so it was listed as "executive assistant.")

"Hi," she says. "I warned you I hate mornings. You can't say I didn't."

"How about some coffee?"

"That would be wonderful."

Sheryl had to be coaxed into just these sorts of outdated secretarial duties, but this new woman, who is old enough to be Judith's mother and has grown-up children of her own, seems bred for caretaking. Judith wasn't surprised that Dolores's last employer was a man, who she imagined expected the fuss and bother as his due. That was the thing about men: they didn't have to worry about appearing peremptory and unsisterly when they made prosaic requests of their female employees.

"Coming right up. How do you like it?"

"Light. No sugar. I really appreciate it, Dolores."

The truth was, Judith has never gotten the hang of being

a boss, even if it was being the boss of just one person. With Sheryl, for instance, she had alternated between making over-friendly gestures and retreating into a chilly sense of hierarchy. Maybe this time around it would be different: she'd be the efficient, vastly admired female boss of a 1940s movie, a mixture of Rosalind Russell and Katharine Hepburn, friendly but in a politely distant sort of way, a model of executive womankind.

"I'll be right back."

"Just a second, please, Dolores, before you go, I was wondering whether there were any calls?"

"Nope. It's been quiet so far this morning. Oops, wait, no, no, someone did call. A woman. Said it wasn't important and she'd try you again later in the day."

"Thank you," Judith says, still standing behind her desk.

Dolores Lawson wore her hair in a stiff, heavily sprayed bouffant and had a gracious, airline-hostess voice. It was the voice that decided Judith when they met briefly in her office for an interview. That, and a certain wryness about her—a sort of arms-folded-across-the-chest, you-can't-fool-me stance toward life—that Judith found appealing. Never mind that Dolores's employment history sounded alarmingly stopgap—a succession of previous jobs had each ended after only a few months—or that she told Judith she wanted her to know right off that spelling was a problem. Thus forewarned, another person who did what Judith did for a living—which depended greatly on the correct use of language—might have been scared off, but not Judith. Dr. Munch's death was still fresh; it hadn't yet had time to seal over, and she was on a reprieve from self-examination. She wanted to be soothed, to be the recipient of someone else's older and wiser views on life; even in the office she looked for a motherly touch close at hand, and Dolores Lawson was motherly in a neutral sort of way: What more could you ask for in a professional setting?

"I told you I needed these to go out yesterday!"

Someone was venting at someone else a few offices down from hers, the voice carrying clearly through the thin partitions. "And now I get a call this morning that he still hasn't received the galleys! Jesus Christ!"

Why, she wondered, was everything in this business of publishing treated as deathly urgent? It was only books, after all, and as anyone who hadn't been living on Mars for the last few decades had to know by now, most of the population didn't read anymore. They had moved on to quicker, more visually gratifying media—to television and the movies—to pass away their leisure hours, leaving book editors to their futile busyness, to screaming about galleys as if Rome were burning.

"Shut up," Judith Stone murmurs, to no one in particular.

On her desk the phone is ringing. She lets it ring three times (no point in appearing too eager) and then picks it up, holding her breath, willing it to be Him. Instead of Howard Rose it is someone she barely knows, Caroline, the younger sister of a friend of Rebecca's, who had invited her to the party on that Saturday night. Casual, lots of people, should be fun, she said.

"Sounds great," Judith had said. "It's so sweet of you to think of me."

Caroline is calling now to explain that she had been meaning to let Judith know that she had given Judith's number recently to a guy she didn't know well named Howard Rose, and that she hoped that was okay, that Judith didn't mind.

"Mind? I should be the one calling you to thank you for inviting me in the first place."

"Well, I'm glad you could come," Caroline goes on sweetly. "And he seemed like an okay guy, although the one I really know is his friend Gayle. He seemed very eager to get in touch with you."

Judith thanks Caroline and reassures her that she was happy to hear from Howard Rose, then gets off the phone before she says any more. Like: *Who is this man? What's his backstory? His history with women? Is he dangerous or just a bit unusual in his approach?* She would love to have Caroline take the burden off her, Judith, to decide for her what was the wise thing to do. For all her sophistication—the way she keeps her ear pinned to the latest rumblings and shifts in the culture, the way she could tell you whom had been written about where and when—Judith suffers from a chronic inability to go forward: not with any conviction, that is. It had taken most of her energy to figure out what to wear to the party and now that she has actually met someone, everything seems murky. She wants children, after all, and she knows enough to look upon this man who has ensnared her heart as a dubious candidate for fatherhood. Not to overlook the fact that getting pregnant didn't seem to be as easy—as automatic—as it once was. Every day she opens the paper to find yet another article on rising infertility rates or on high-tech methods of inducing pregnancy in recalcitrant wombs. If she doesn't hurry, she'll find herself going to a sperm bank in her late thirties and making a withdrawal.

Meanwhile, she puts her feet up on her desk, pulls a file folder marked "Urgent" toward herself, and stares past it into the middle distance, where Howard Rose lies in wait.

XII

"ARE YOU COMING?" he asks, gliding in and out of her, smooth as can be, his penis slick with her juices.

"I don't know," she says.

The room they are in is dark; it might as well be night, although it is late Sunday afternoon. His blinds are closed against the lingering light, and Judith feels as if they have been doing this for hours, as if she has lost track of time. It is exactly two weeks to the day that the man named Howard Rose first called her, after the party. This is the third time they have made love since he picked her up at her building the first time, sporting a white silk scarf thrown loosely around his neck. Judith had been struck by the dashing sartorial touch; she hadn't expected it, given his taste in shoes.

"You feel very wet," he says. "Like you're enjoying me fucking you."

She inhales his smell, a mixture of Old Spice (it is oddly familiar to her, this cologne, and she realizes that she has smelled it frequently in passing, on taxi drivers and on the super in her building and on boys she knew in high school) and other, more pungent odors. She had thought of buying him a less common cologne, like Dunhill—a subtle, unexpected choice, indicating due respect for his singular masculinity. But that was at the very beginning, in that brief period when it still seems possible to remake the other person, and in the end she had decided against it. For all she knew, he would be insulted, take it as a criticism.

"I want you to come," he says. "I want to feel you come."

"I don't know if I ever have," she says. "*You* come."

"No," he says, "not if you don't."

Howard Rose has enormous staying power and what Judith supposes would be called a nice penis. (Although the whole notion of assessing a man's sexual equipment has always struck her as vulgar—hardly to be admitted even to herself, in spite of the fact that men judged women all the time without feeling in the least compromised.)

"I don't know," she says again. "Maybe I've never come. I can't tell for sure."

He pulls out of her suddenly, leaving her gaping.

"What is it? What's wrong?"

She wants him back inside, filling her up, thrusting against the walls of her being, breaking them down.

"Nothing," he says.

"Why'd you stop?"

Judith leans over and nuzzles his neck. She can hear his watch ticking, then the sounds from the street—a truck rumbling noisily by, a woman screaming "Get ovah here *now!*"—and she feels as though the world is back in the room with them, reasserting its claims upon their attention.

"Because."

"Does it bother you?"

"What?"

"My not coming."

"No."

He sounds disgusted, or disinterested, she can't tell which. She can't see his eyes. He is flat on his back, staring at the ceiling, removed from her.

"I should've known," he adds.

"Known what?"

She wants him to play with her breasts again, to come back to her, not to leave her in the lurch.

"That you'd be a piece of work."

"Meaning?"

"Fucked-up."

He has curled over toward the window, away from her. On the left side of his back, down low, near his hip, he has a mole— more delicate than a mole, a beauty mark, really—which she notices now for the first time. It occurs to her that if he were to die unexpectedly, be shot down by a stray bullet, or keel over on the subway from a fatal heart attack, she would be able to identify his corpse by this mark.

"Fucked-up about what?"

"Sex. Everything. Women like you always are."

She is sitting up now, her back rigid against his uncomfortable wooden headboard. Judith Stone privately considered the whole issue of female orgasm to be a vastly overrated one. All that fuss over Freud and his misbegotten hierarchies of normal female sexual development! She could see how he had been wrong in valuing the vaginal over the clitoral variety of orgasm, but she doubted whether half the women she knew could tell the difference—could tell whether they were having a real, true-blue orgasm at all, if they were being honest about it. She remembered reading somewhere that roughly fifty percent of American women had them, which confirmed her private sense of things. Men had it so much easier in that respect, with their telltale physiology, their uninteriorized erotic symptoms: all those unmistakable hard-ons and ejaculations, the semen shooting its viscous film, there was nothing vague or mysterious about it.

"I suppose," she says angrily, "you have no problems at all. Men like you never do."

"At least I know I like to fuck," he says.

"So do baboons," she says.

Judith wonders to herself whether it was possible to be born without a sense of pleasure. Like being born without a sense of taste or smell . . . a small but radical difference in human composition. It seemed plausible.

"You've got to let go," he says, his voice gone soft and coaxing all of a sudden. "Didn't you ever trust anybody? Any man? Your daddy? Your older brother?"

"I don't have an older brother," she says, avoiding the whole issue of her father. "And besides which," she doesn't say, "you'd be the last person I'd trust. As a matter of fact, I think you're

crazy, but you're very disciplined so it's hard to see your crazi-
ness. Your moods turn on a dime and I think you hate women
but I'm drawn to moody men who hate women so I think about
you all the time."

"Trust me," he says quite simply.

"I could try."

Could it be that she was just too sad for unalloyed sexual
gratification?

"Thatta girl," he says. And then: "I've got an idea."

"What?"

"You'll see. Turn over on your stomach."

Howard Rose arranges her body in what is a new configura-
tion for her, her face against his pillow, her ass propped up high.
Then, stroking her all the while, caressing her buttocks, he enters her from behind. It strikes Judith as the perfect position, an
antidote to self-consciousness: his penis filling her up facelessly,
leaving her free to roam among a range of responses without
being observed. She feels a rush go through her body, and then
another, a sensation like no other. Why this, she thinks, must be
what all the fuss was about, the fifty percent lording it over the
rest of unawakened womankind.

"Do I own you now?"

Out of breath and sweaty, as though she's just been vaulting
high fences, and not quite sure what he means by the question
but liking its territorial insistence, she says: "Yes."

Now she has turned back around, facing him, and he pulls
her down on the bed. "Do I?" he asks again, kissing her, his tongue
swilling in her mouth.

"Yes," she says again, limp with pleasure.

Afterward—it is evening in earnest now, and they have lain in bed talking pleasantly and he has gotten up and played a favorite jazz tape (he is opposed to CDs, says there is no stopping the greed of the American marketplace or gullibility of the American consumer)—they take a bath together. It is the first time she has taken a bath as a grown-up woman with a grown-up man, two adults splashing around. They sit facing each other, companionable, her smooth-shaven legs nested inside his long, hairy ones. He has a windup toy sitting on the ledge of the tub, a green plastic turtle. She watches as he sends it spinning across the water, cheering it on, and wonders what his childhood was like.

"Thatta boy," Howard Rose says encouragingly, "slow but steady wins the race." The turtle chugs across the tub to the other side, where it sputters and spins, then bobs upside down in the water.

"Men and their toys," she says affectionately.

"Do you want me to wash your back?" he asks.

She turns around awkwardly in the tub and sits on her knees, mindful that he is getting to see her body from all angles, the slight bulge of her belly. He soaps her gently with a washcloth and a bar of Dial soap. She scoots back around and watches as he lathers himself, then takes her hand and places it on his penis, which turns stiff in the warm water.

"Kiss it," he says.

"I don't know," she says, stalling for time, the water lapping between her thighs. She is used to doing this in the dark, without being observed.

He gets up on his knees and pulls her to hers.

"Put it in your mouth," he says, pushing his penis toward her. "Please."

Suddenly it seems clear to her that Howard Rose is eminently worthy of her trust, after all. He is just a little boy playing with his bath toys, a little boy with watchful eyes come to take her hand and show her places she's never been. His bathtub is very clean and there are nice blue towels—a little worn, but the generous size she likes—for them to wrap themselves in afterward. What has she been so worried about? Judith Stone leans over and puts him in her mouth, her lips circling the buttery tip.

DIGRESSION #3

BACK TO YOU, *mon semblable, mon frère, mon cher lecteur,* or whatever it was Charles Baudelaire called his readers. Elegant language, French, in spite of the fact that it seems to be the foreign language of choice for the children of socially aspiring American parents. A little French, *ma petite? Mais oui, maman, mais oui!* All the same, wish I knew it better: years of past participles and pluperfects in high school, then countless more irregular verbs in college, and I still brighten when I can actually understand a string of words at a French movie without consulting the subtitles . . .

But as for Baudelaire: now there's another mother-fixated poet for you. I've often wondered whether all the best male writers and artists—those, at least, of a certain stripe, like Gustave Flaubert and Édouard Vuillard—are mother-stuck. In other words, to borrow from the title of the late, great critic Edmund Wilson's disquisition on the making of artistic identity, *The Wound and the Bow*: Without the wound of mother-stuckness, would there be any need to develop the supple bow of creative endeavor? We could all just sit home and watch reruns instead. Or does that sound too Freudian for you? Just some more gobbledygook about traumatic childhoods, when what we want is to get past the goddamned childhood, isn't it?

But look, I'm so tired of trying to pretend this is a book I'm writing, something out there that's printed and bound, when it's merely something fleeting and delicately constituted in here—no more, that is, than some dialogue and observations and descriptions (can't forget those all-important descriptions) I keep plucking out of my head. Howard Rose as the demon lover, the Black Knight indeed! For all you know (as long as we're dabbling in hypothetical constructs), Judith Stone really had the upper hand the whole time and just didn't realize it.

You must have noticed by now how I keep trying to sneak past you on my way in and out of describing her, Judith Stone (my alter ego, flawed for accuracy's sake, but fetchingly so) and her love affair. Tell you what: How about we drop all the convoluted literary devices for the moment and concentrate wholly on you? For the occasion of which I'll try on my cozy southern waitress voice, just for the fun of it. Ready? Here goes: How you doin' today, honey? Did you get some nice grits inside you this mornin'? How about 'nother cup of coffee? Comin' right up. Lookin' real gray and nasty out there today, don't it?

Now imagine that this very waitress—Lucy, say (notice how much easier it is to summon up a person, even a character in a novel whom you've never met and never will meet, once he or she has a name)—is chatting away, pencil behind her ear, order pad in her apron pocket, to a man sitting in a booth, reading *The New York Times*, a man who happens to look like a dead ringer for Howard Rose. Without having read this book I keep trying to write, would she have the vaguest idea that this man with a trim dark beard, sallow skin, and wounded eyes ("like someone hurt him long ago," is how Lucy puts it to herself) is an object of sexual obsession? Or would she pass him over as an intense-looking lawyer type who comes in regular-like, none too talky, always orders the same thing for breakfast, steady as rain, a fairly good tipper, not the best, but better than average.

What I'm trying to get to, in my own way, is what drew Judith Stone to Howard Rose, whom he reminded her of, the echoes he evoked. The question, in more general terms, is this: Without preconceptions, where are we?

Answer: Lost in the world with no one to call our own, no one to call up echoes of the past. What's precious to you is likely to be forgettable to me, and vice versa, unless we have had remarkably similar experiences long ago. By this I mean a profound level of shared experiences: how it felt to sit on your mother's lap when she didn't put her arms around you, or the way in which bathroom functions were handled in your family—cleanliness and smells and shitting. (Have you ever noticed, by the way, how people tend to marry spouses with a like level of cleanliness? Or if they don't, how this disparity can in and of itself rend the marriage asunder? I think this is an interesting, insufficiently cited aspect of married life: if changing the sheets before a guest arrives is important to one-half of a couple, it's usually important to the other as well. You rarely get a marriage where the husband showers twice a day and the wife has oily hair, or one in which he has the ability to overlook the smell of dirty diapers and she doesn't; either they both do or they both don't.)

What most of us have in common, when you come right down to it, is precious little: a grab bag of cultural goodies, your having once loved Bazooka bubble gum or Saul Bellow, or *Jeopardy!* It has nothing to do with the pulsating rhythms of interior life—which hearken back, whether you like it or not, to those echoes from childhood. Small wonder we're all so lonely sitting back here among the dusty trappings of our lives, our husbands, and dirty clothes in the hamper and unread copies of magazines, watching other people fall madly in love with the man we overlooked. No wonder we're all so bitten through with envy and longing, watching other people dance in the sun as we skulk in the shadows.

Go ahead, tell me you're not an envious sort. That it's only me, passing by a bookstore window featuring a new novel by someone I know slightly, who responds by feeling ill with jealousy. This happened a mere two days ago: I walked past a bookstore and there she was, smiling from her jacket photo, triumphant as can be, piles of her new novel artfully displayed for all the world to see. Her first novel, reissued in resplendent paperback to coincide with the hardcover publication of her new one, also eating up window space. Why her? And not me? Rumor has it that she has admirably disciplined writing habits, is at her desk every morning by eight o'clock. Not like some people I could name who cultivate distraction, will meet you for lunch at

the drop of a hat, and in general meander about the city searching for ways not to work.

So there I am, standing in front of the window, cut by lash-
ings of self-disgust, when I seize upon the following consola-
tion, if only to spare my own smarting hide: her book's too
long! We're no longer living in the age of Dickens and serial-
ized installments, after all, and you can't presume too much on
people's time. Even the book-loving people I know barely get
to books these days, they're so busy just keeping up. Anything
much over three hundred pages—350 tops—and my own spirits
start to flag. Five hundred pages, I tell myself, she's shot herself
in the leg right there! Okay, go ahead, tell me you're not an envious sort, and I won't believe you. Everyone has a green spot in
their heart where someone else—less talented or kind or loyal
or dogged, less worthy in every way than you—treads, causing spasms of pain.

The problem of envy is endemic, I think, to being alive. And
for some women (trust me on this one), it's endemic to being
less thin than another woman, one who can wear the clothes
of summer—those light, body-revealing, seasonally correct
clothes—better than they can. Where will you hide twenty-five
extra pounds once the disguises of winter get put away? There is
nothing so desirable, from a heavy woman's standpoint, as thin-
ness. When you envision Judith Stone I want you to see her as I
was: my sublime alter ego, flawed for accuracy, as I mentioned
earlier, but fetchingly so, not an ounce overweight, for God's
sake.

I promise not to digress much longer, but I just have to tell you how hard it can get spinning out this novel, my can of Diet Coke beside me, gamely trying to ignore the demons of doubt and futility. What every writer needs is not an audience but a personal in-house cheerleader, someone with a plummy voice and great conviction, someone gifted at uniting warring factions in the face of a larger task: Churchill exhorting the British during World War II; or JFK, standing in the snow at his inauguration, sowing the seeds of amity in his dry, Boston-accented cadences. Ask not what your reader can do for you, ask what you can do for your reader.

So tell me, *mon cher* reader, *mon hypocrite lecteur*, to come back to that unmasterable language: How much do I reveal without revealing more than you want to know? Do you want, for instance, a glimpse of Judith as a young girl? A scene of her lying in her childhood bed, in the room she shared with her sister, reading *Half Magic*, or *Rowena Carey*, or a few years later, a much-loved "young adult" novel with the strikingly belligerent title *Don't Call Me Katie Rose*? Or how about a few peeks at the just bar-mitzvahed Howard, still practicing his left-handed pitch, before he hardened into his adult self? A full-bodied description of the buildings they each live in? His with a doorman, hers without? I wish I were writing a biography, could overwhelm you with the research I've carefully accumulated on index cards. If I pelt you with information—the color of the carpet in her bedroom, the way he bought canned tomato sauce and then doctored it up at home, adding diced onions and carrots and tons of garlic—will you feel you've gotten your money's worth?

Writers are like wily children born into large families,

hounded by siblings, forever trying to capture your attention. I think of someone leaving this book out in the sun, its pages stained with soda, crumbs caught in the binding. Is that you? Bored or distracted or busy, you will inevitably set this book down and go off to other claims: the phone ringing, a child crying, dinner to be cooked. Perhaps you are not the reader I want after all.

XIII

ON A MONDAY MORNING in mid-June, Judith can be found in the conference room, where the weekly editorial meeting of Phoenix Books is taking place around a long oval table, with yellow legal pads, sharpened pencils, and Styrofoam cups of coffee at the ready. This is where Dolores Lawson finds her and, after knocking on the door and interrupting a heated discussion about a book proposal on a recently deceased film director, hands her a note with the words "URGENT PHONE CALL" written on it in neat capital letters. Judith nods at Dolores and gestures that she'll come out and take the call.

"I don't see that many copies," Steven, the company's bearded wunderkind marketing director, is saying. "I see thousands of books coming back if we were to begin to print anywhere near that number of copies."

"Excuse me," Judith says, pushing her chair back from the table. Her shoulder bag, which she has hung from the chair, falls to the floor. Katrina, who is sitting on her right, her trademark perfume wafting its green scent through the room (causing Judith to wonder irritably, not for the first time, why anyone would want to smell like a freshly cut lawn), looks up from her doodling.

"Auf Wiedersehen," she says blackly. Katrina is fluent in several languages, having spent much of her childhood in foreign schools as the daughter of a diplomat.

"He's a cult figure, for God's sake," Steven is continuing. "And not even an American cult figure! Most of the country hasn't heard of him."

"No one ever went broke underestimating the intelligence of the American people, isn't that right, Steve?"

"I don't know about that, Cal," the marketing director says, rubbing the side of his face thoughtfully. "I just know this one doesn't feel that big to me. I can't see us getting in an auction and losing our cool over it, put it that way."

"Mencken," Katrina says dryly. "If you're going to quote Mencken at Steve, Cal, at least give him credit."

Cal Anderson—the Cal was short for Robert (the nickname didn't make sense to Judith, the only other person she had ever heard of with this same bewildering nickname was Robert Lowell)—gives a brief, weary smile. He and Katrina, editorial director and senior editor, respectively, considered themselves to be the standard-bearers of high culture in an increasingly low-brow industry and as such were given to competitive attributions of great sayings and esoteric phrases.

"Excuse me," Judith says again, standing behind her chair. "I've got to take this call. I just want to say that I liked it, for whatever it's worth. I thought it got into the granular details of moviemaking in a way I hadn't read before. The agent sent it to me on an exclusive and I promised I'd let her know by the end of the day."

"Granular." She had chosen the word deliberately, just to keep them on their toes.

"I read it," Elaina says, and then pauses.

Shit. Leave it to Elaina to pick this moment to weigh in with her usual defeatist opinion. The subsidiary-rights manager of Phoenix spent much of her day reading magazines with her feet up on the desk, and you could count on her to always underestimate the potential value of a book in paperback and foreign sales. Still, it was politic for an editor who was excited about a book to show it to her, if only to get an idea just how naysaying she'd be about the book's prospects. The one editor who was lucky enough to bypass her was Jane Moss, who specialized in books on birds and English gardens.

"Frankly, I don't see that much softcover interest," Elaina continues in her disarming, correct-me-if-I'm-wrong manner. "Although I see where Judith might be excited. I've always been an admirer of Frank Medavoy's early films, and his influence on the younger generation of directors has been enormous, of course, but I don't know how many of us there actually are. In other words: Who's the reader?"

In other words: Shut up, Judith thinks to herself as she heads back to her office. She found it hard to believe that anyone bought into Elaina's fake sweetness or her pseudo-erudition, but both Cal and Steve were die-hard believers in her dark view of the marketplace. At moments like these she feels nostalgic for her graduate school days, the two years she spent discussing the colonialist impulse in Isak Dinesen's construction of self, or the transgressive streak in Nabokov's fiction.

Once upon a time she had wanted to become a professor, had imagined writing a PhD dissertation that would analyze the symbiotic romantic attachments among three strong women and the men who drove them either mad or to suicide. She had taken notes galore, as was her habit, and had come up with a theory on the correlation between female creative aggression and the need to disown it by engaging in a relationship with a more dominant man. She saw herself becoming a much sought-after teacher, her name established as an original and controversial thinker. But she had dropped out of graduate school after two years and had only gotten as far as writing an unfinished master's thesis on the conflict between the desire for love and the desire for selfhood in the characters of women writers from George Eliot to Virginia Woolf. What had happened to her? Instead of analyzing these predicaments she was now living them.

"Let's take it up again when Judith comes back," Steven says. "Meanwhile, let's move on, okay?"

Outside in the hall Judith notices that the ancient half-slip she has grabbed from the back of a drawer is showing and rolls it up under her waistband. She wonders whether everyone has noticed and whether they are all talking about her now that she has left the room. She had read somewhere that Trotsky— Trotsky or some other Communist leader, she can't remember exactly who—was promptly voted out of power when he left a Party meeting for a few minutes. Which went to show that it was dangerous to bow out of meetings, and that you could never trust anyone, not even your allies. She was probably being thrown to the dogs right now.

Back in her office and seated at her desk, she picks up the phone.

"Hello?"

"Stone. Rose here. What the fuck took you so long? I've been holding this phone for hours."

Her heart starts beating faster, as if on cue, and then the familiar tom-tom starts up, lower down.

"I was in a meeting."

"Fuck that," he says.

"Fuck fuck fuck," she says. "Your favorite word. What's so urgent?"

"You. I want to fuck you."

"That's nice," she says calmly, but deep down she recognizes she is ready to give up everything—her authors, her biweekly paychecks, her lunch appointments, her friends, the very hum of her life—everything, at his impetuous command.

"What you doing tonight, my little chickadee?"

"Why?"

"I want to make you come again."

"Howard," she says, "can anyone hear you?"

"Only my whole office. We're on speakerphone."

"Very funny," she says.

"I've been thinking," he says, "how to make you come more efficiently. I want you to buck like a horse under my skilled reins."

Was he making fun of himself? She couldn't tell but she didn't think so; his sense of humor didn't seem to include his own laughable aspects. He was a strange sort, for sure, but was there another man alive who would pay her such heady attention? She feels an unexpected swell of gratitude. Howard Rose had known her less than a month and was already applying himself to the study of her erotic core—which was opaque even to her—with greater concentration than any man she had ever met: he seemed to regard her sexuality as a code he alone could crack. After which he would possess her forever: it was hyperbolic but true.

"You're not talking, Stone. Do you need more reasons? Do you want me to tell you that I like your high cheekbones? And your ass? Because I do, it's a nice, round ass, a classic of its kind. I hate broad-beamed women, if you know what I mean."

"I do," she says, curiously delighted by his connoisseurship. Then, conscious of selling her whole sex down the river for the sake of aligning herself with him, she adds: "I hate them, too."

He chuckles mirthlessly. Howard Rose had the least joyful laugh she had ever heard. It wasn't as though he didn't appreciate the comic side of things; he could be quite funny, in fact. But he seemed to have developed a sense of humor in a vacuum, alone in his boyhood room, under cover of darkness; there was something masturbatory about his laugh.

"So," he says, as casually as though they've been discussing the weather, "I've gotta run. Talk to you later."

"Wait," she says.

"What is it?"

His voice had turned hard again, impenetrable. One minute

he was chasing her into the labyrinth of her innermost self, and the next he was banging the phone down, severing their connection. It occurs to her yet again that she would be nuts to give herself up to a man this volatile; he would possess her only to prove a point—after which she would be left flapping in the breeze, discarded. Perhaps it wasn't desire at all but some sort of death wish, a means of jumping over the fence of her too-familiar life into the bottomless pit of erotic self-abandon. This isn't the first time the thought has occurred to her—indeed she has discussed it with Celia more than once—but she would need a Dr. Munch to sort out all its implications.

"Howard," she says urgently.

"I've got people waiting for me," he says.

"Howard," she says again.

But what is it she wants to say? Outside her office Dolores is typing, phones are ringing, a company meeting is in progress, which she should be attending. On the other end of the phone is a man who talks to her like no man she has ever known, who is interested in her in a way no one else has ever been.

"I was wondering, do you think this will work out?"

"What?"

"Us."

"Betcha bottom dollar. If you don't fuck it up first. Which you might. Ball's in your court."

What she had wanted to ask was this: *Do you love me?* But it was too much too soon, she'd scare him clear away, although in truth it was hard to tell how he'd react.

"Bye," she says, trying to sound decisive.

"You might think," he says, "about telling me you love me madly." And then, quite deliberately, before she has a chance to answer, he hangs up.

He knew. Not only did he know but it didn't scare him. There was no place to go but further in. You could plan your whole life around a revolution of the proletariat and then look what happened when you walked out of the room for a minute. She'd take her chances.

XIV

"TELL ME WHERE IT HURTS," the doctor says, one hand on her belly (she contracts her stomach muscle immediately at his touch, hoping it will work like stage magic to undo any extra pounds), the other ready to go inside of her and root out the problem.

Judith Stone lifts the upper half of her body from where she is reclining on the examining table and looks at the gynecologist, standing way down the other end, framed by her feet in the stirrups. She is shrouded in one of those uncomfortable papery robes that open in the back, with a crudely cut-out neck and armholes like a child's drawing. She wonders why her doctor doesn't stock regular cotton robes, the way Celia's gynecologist does. According to Celia, there are pale peach robes, and bottles of perfume in the bathroom, as well. Such indulgences struck her as suspect, somehow: "Sounds like a spa, not a doctor's office," she had sniffed, but as she lies here in Dr. Glickman's cold, well-lit examining room, efficient to the point of barrenness, she thinks she could do with a soft, cosseting touch or two.

"Tell me where," he says again. She stares up at the ceiling, into the harsh fluorescent light.

"In my vaginal area," she says primly.

She wonders if she could be in pain from having too-frequent sex, whether her vaginal walls have collapsed in protest against the constant ramming they've been subjected to. But she knows better than raising this possibility, knows even as she thinks it that there is something medieval about the image, something borrowed from scenarios of war rather than lovemaking.

Dr. Glickman stands up and pushes his glasses back on his nose—a straightforward tortoiseshell pair, as befits a doctor or lawyer. He proceeds to take off his examining glove, rolling the cream-colored latex down his hand, the one that has been inside of her seconds ago, with a snap: when he pulls the glove off, it looks spent, like a used condom. Judith likes to watch these clean movements of his, the way he pulls on the glove by holding his hand upright while he dexterously works the material—so thin and supple it fits like a transparent second skin—over his fingers, then flexes his hand several times to check the fit.

The matter-of-factness of gynecologists' offices, their complete lack of visual discretion, never fails to give her a jolt: There is a perforated box of these gloves, a tube of lubricating jelly, and a speculum on a standing steel tray, and several feet farther back is a plain white Formica counter (she imagines Celia's doctor's office done up in delicate coral shades) featuring some small, medicinal-looking bottles and a large box of cotton.

Displayed on a stand of its own for all to see is a graduated series of diaphragms, arrayed like hubcaps in a gas station. She finds it difficult to envision Dr. Glickman fitting out all manner and size of women with these contraceptive devices, big women with astonishingly small insides and slender women built unexpectedly wide across the cervix. She herself had been fitted once, several years ago, by a different doctor, but has never gotten around to using the diaphragm. She prefers the lottery of unprotected sex, knowing how little chance there is, given her perennially late periods—not to mention her diagnosis some years back of polycystic ovaries, which she completely ignored—that she will get pregnant without medical intervention.

"It's nothing to get alarmed about," Dr. Glickman says. "It's a simple case of vaginitis. Hard to say at this point if it's something to keep an eye out for in the future, but right now it should be perfectly treatable. I'll prescribe you some medication that should heal it pretty quickly. I'll leave the prescription for you at the desk."

He pauses for a moment, this man of professional enterprise, in his crisp white coat, acknowledging her presence. Sitting there on the edge of the examining table, her bare legs dangling, Judith suddenly wants to ask him—as she wants to ask everyone she comes into contact with—for clues to the art of living. "How do you do it, Dr. Glickman, go about this business of setting up a life?" In his case she supposed it must have been a fairly linear process—a matter of making plans and then of following through on them: eating the solid meals his mother undoubtedly prepared for him; studying hard to get good grades;

applying to medical school; graduating medical school; getting married; choosing an address for his practice, then furnishing the office, deciding carefully on the couches and pictures to hang on the wall. She wondered whether it was his wife, doubling as a decorator, who had suggested the gray and burgundy motif in the reception area, the gentle prints of ducks and horses. Maybe he fancied himself a country squire? She knows he likes to sail on weekends but other than that she knows little about him.

"There's nothing to worry about," Judith repeats after him. "I understand. I tend to ignore these things altogether, except that it's been bothering me a lot. But I mean, why did it suddenly pop up?"

"It can happen out of the blue like this," Dr. Glickman says, "without apparent cause. I wouldn't worry. You seem fine otherwise."

He stands with one hand on the doorknob; tucked under his other arm is a file folder that he has plucked from a plastic holder affixed to the outside of the door of the examining room. There is the same folder, of a varying thickness, for each patient—filled, she assumes, with the methodical, brief notations of visits past, the relevant bits and pieces of gynecological information: late menarche, for instance, or: history of missed periods, or: ovarian cancer in mother's family, and on and on, dispassionately charting the rise and inevitable fall of the female body, the moist excitement of puberty ending in gray pubic hairs and dropped body parts.

"You should be back to scratch within ten days, especially if you hold off on sexual relations in the meantime. Call me in a week to let me know how you're feeling," the doctor says. "Sooner if you continue to have discomfort."

He pushes back his hair from his forehead and gives her a concluding smile. Judith suddenly notices the faint smell of his aftershave, bracing and dry. She can tell that in his mind he's already moved on to the next file folder, the next female in a crude paper gown. Dr. Glickman is all done with her; she's someone else's concern now.

"Thank you," she says, smiling back. It is a Thursday morning, Judith Stone has a case of vaginitis, and she does not ask the following questions: Will I be able to have children? Will someone ever love me enough to want to marry me? Why did you marry your wife? Does she ever get vaginal infections? Is this small bodily glitch a reflection of a larger problem? Is anything really wrong with me, Doc?

"Have a good day," he says, and then, shifting into a chattier manner, a less expedient form of personal communication, Dr. Glickman adds: "You're looking well. Something must be agreeing with you." And then he is gone, leaving behind his brisk forest smell.

She gets dressed, first pulling on her underpants, then moving on to her bra, which she fastens back to front. She has never gotten the hang of hooking her bra in the back, the way other women seem able to do, shifting their bodies slightly forward to scoop their breasts into the cups and then neatly enclosing them. Judith thinks it must have something to do with the size of her breasts, preventing a graceful front-to-back motion; or perhaps it is simply a native ineptitude. More troubling is the fact that she still thinks of her body as being divided along some invisible demarcation line into two separate areas—"top" and "bottom." This infection of hers resides somewhere in the vast uncharted region of her "bottom," which ends in the approximate vicinity of her waist. Above her waist begins the topography of her "top," which includes her breasts and, of course, her head and all its contents.

"Dr. Glickman wants you to fill this right away."

Sylvia, the receptionist, hands her a prescription across which the doctor has scrawled his impenetrable hieroglyphics. No self-respecting doctor Judith knew of deigned to write in a legible script.

"Thanks," Judith says.

"You want us to mail you the bill?"

"Please."

She had to hand it to Dr. Glickman and his staff—the trusty Sylvia, and the near-silent nurse, Marsha, who flitted shadowlike around the examining room, attesting by her watchful presence to the doctor's moral probity: it was an altogether well-run, if slightly inhuman office.

"Take care now," Sylvia says, rolling back in her chair to her computer, where she begins to type with alarming speed.

"Thanks," Judith says again. All this rigid politeness was exhausting. With automaton-like sincerity Sylvia volleys back: "Have a good day."

Out on the street Judith puts her hand up for a taxi. She is not in the mood for the subway, for the noise and dirt and indifference. She feels threatened by the prospect of her own anonymity, stirred up by her visit to Dr. Glickman. The ease with which she falls into a state of nonbeing, the human equivalent of a widget, has always struck her as odd; she wonders whether other people feel similarly or whether this is a vulnerability peculiar to her. It was one of the things that made her ripe for the picking by one such as Howard, makes her willing to cede him vast portions of herself in return for his utmost attention.

Somewhere, somehow, Judith had missed out on the feeling of safety that you were supposed to get as an infant. She had discussed it with Dr. Munch time and time over, her sense that her mother was not, when you came right down to it, the maternal type. Her interest in Judith had been mercurial at best, with the result that Judith had never reached that crucial point of independence where you learn to look out for yourself. To this day what she wants more than anything else in the world is what she wanted as a child, which was not to be a separate person, a sovereign self, but to live inside someone else's pocket, like a baby kangaroo.

Dr. Munch had tried to address this still-resonant lack every which way: "You want to be cared for when you need to care for yourself," he had opined, or "You keep hoping that if you try hard enough you'll find what wasn't there to begin with." Perhaps if they could have continued working together—if he hadn't died—she would now be a healthier specimen, a woman who avoided men who cut you no slack, who asked things such as "Do I own you now?" after a heated round of sex. (Although, of course, it was this very quality of being captive to someone else's will that drew her into Howard's web in the first place.) Now that Dr. Munch is gone forever, all she has is Howard Rose and his curious, now-you-see-it, now-you-don't embrace. Although she can't be sure that what is on offer is anything more than sex, the intermittent hothouse quality of his focus on her feels like something close to love.

XV

"I'D BE INTERESTED," Judith Stone is saying, fiddling with the crusty little jawbreaker of a roll that is on her bread plate, "in anything she'd want to write about. And so would the rest of her fans."

"I'll let her know," the agent says, over the din and clatter of the restaurant. "Although I imagine it'll be hard to convince her she has anything to say. The two ghostwriters who were sent to her last year struck out because they came on too strong. We'll have to be very careful about how we approach her."

"Understood," Judith says, leaning over the table, offering up her intensity as a pledge.

"She's strangely modest in that way," the agent is going on, his eyes focused somewhere behind her. "She believes that her chosen craft of acting is enough. She doesn't fully get the drift of things these days. I've explained to her that the talk shows would kill to have her on and that alone would guarantee the success of any memoir she'd care to put her name to."

"Will she discuss the husbands?"

"Some of them."

A waiter hovers into view, offering to replenish their coffee.

"No more for me, thanks. How about you?"

The agent, Dan Foley, a native midwesterner whose easy style and boyish features can't quite disguise his steely purposefulness, passes on the coffee as well and Judith asks for the check.

"Circus life?"

"Excuse me?"

She has been off somewhere else for a second or two, thinking of possibly indulging in some sexy underwear, momentarily tired of generating enthusiasm for this memoir-to-be by an aging actress that the whole country is purportedly awaiting. She was a good listener, everyone told her so, although at least half the time at these business lunches she found herself in a state of suppressed incredulity. It was like a rain dance to gods she didn't really believe in, this buying and selling of books: it didn't begin to resemble her college courses in literature, those earnest discussions of the novel of sensibility—Virginia Woolf and her suicidal stand-ins—versus, say, George Eliot's novels of social criticism, the bustling microcosm of *Middlemarch*. Judith had always preferred the novel of sensibility herself, limited in scope as it was, but what did that say about her? Maybe she was unfit for the real world, like Septimus in *Mrs. Dalloway*, who was privy to the secret conversations of birds and died a suicide.

"She began her acting career in the circus," the agent is saying. "Maybe that would be the right pitch."

"Sounds intriguing," Judith says, sipping distractedly at the tepid remnants of her coffee. "I know so little about circus life. Was she an acrobat?"

"Something like that," Dan Foley says. "Something colorful."

The bill arrives, an astronomical amount given how little they've eaten. She could stock her entire kitchen for a month with what they've just spent on two small pieces of fish, a few sprigs of parsley, a grilled tomato apiece, a bottle of sparkling water, and two cups of coffee.

"Anything the matter?"

"No, no," Judith says. Expense account or not, she can't get out of the habit of adding up the charges in her head. She signs the bill quickly and takes her copy. "We're all set."

"Well," the agent says, pushing back his chair, "I guess it's back to the salt mines."

Outside the sky is a bright blue, and there is a light breeze.

"Kite-flying weather," Dan Foley observes, surprising her. She took him for one of those remorseless carpe diem types— too geared up for the opportunities of the present to give a thought to the past. But here he is, lapsing into nostalgia: "I used to fly them every chance I got when I was a kid. Makes me want to play hooky."

"Sounds like fun," Judith says absently.

"If I weren't in such a rush, I'd walk. It's so nice out. But I've got an auction to get back to. Can I drop you in a cab?"

"I think we're in opposite directions."

"Right, you're farther downtown, I forget," the agent says, chuckling. "I still think of you at the old address in the Fifties."

"Keep me posted on any developments, will you?" Judith says, sounding a brisk but convivial note.

"You bet."

They pump each other's hands with uncalled-for enthusiasm and then Judith walks out into one of the city's rare, picture-perfect summer days.

XVI

BACK IN the refrigerated climate of her office—the air con-ditioner is going at full throttle; she keeps meaning to check why the thermostat can't be set to a more reasonable, un-teeth-chattering level—Judith puts her head down on her desk. Why, she wondered, did she have to work at all? And in an office with sealed windows, moreover, so that you could never catch a breath of fresh air, even in idyllic weather like this. What she wants right now is to be lying on a beach next to Howard Rose, turning brown in the sun in her black one-piece (she'd always preferred the subtle eroticism of a one-piece to the soft porn of a bikini), the faintly chemical perfume of suntan lotion on her warm skin, the seagulls cawing around them, looking forward to being explored by him. He continues to surprise her in that way, the passion he directed at every lowly appendage of hers; the last time he had undertook to kiss her toes—devoutly almost, each and every one.

"Excuse me?"

It is Roxanne, from publicity, standing tentatively in the doorway.

"I didn't see Dolores out there, so I thought I'd check if you were in."

"I am," Judith says. "Unhappily."

"Is this a bad time?"

"No, no. Perfect. I just got back from lunch."

Roxanne is of a breed that Judith doesn't understand—a breed endemic to the promotional end of book publishing: literal-minded, even-tempered, well-dressed. She seemed to approach books as though they were horses to be groomed, trained, mounted, and then driven hard to the finish line.

"Cal thought I should go over the tour plans for *Misty's Children* with you."

"Great."

Misty's Children was a saga, set in the early twentieth century, about an Irish maid-in-waiting who rose above great adversity to become a duchess. It was set to come out in the fall, up against the big guns, the new Tom Clancy and Robert Ludlum and Danielle Steel. Fall meant you were serious about your expectations, although spring and summer books had more chance of being noticed. Advertising money was being lavished on *Misty's Children*, and in-house hopes for its success were high. Even Elaina had allowed that she might be able to generate enthusiasm for it. In truth it was Judith's least favorite book; she had acquired it from one of the city's more powerful agents as an indication of her ability to spot and reel in a glittering catch, but it was just the sort of unabashedly commercial project the publicity and marketing departments relished.

"I've got all the material here."

Roxanne spread her papers out on Judith's desk, drawing attention to her well-tended hands.

"Do I spot some new jewelry?"

Roxanne fingers one of her many rings—a wide gold band engraved with hieroglyphic-like markings, then holds her right, perfectly manicured hand in the air and gazes upon it appreciatively.

"I couldn't resist it. What do you think? Cool, isn't it?"

Judith hated people over the age of twenty-one who used "cool" as a descriptive adjective; it set her teeth on edge.

"Beautiful," Judith says, thinking to herself how she always sounded formal—elderly, even—compared to Roxanne, even though the publicist is only three years her junior. "And these bookings are spectacular. How'd you manage to send her to all these places?"

"Yup," Roxanne says. "We've done a great job, if I say so myself. That 'Danielle Steel with an edge' line seems to work like a charm, especially when they see the photos. We're still working on *Oprah*."

Susannah Woods, budding best-selling author, had the sort of hyperfeminine looks—long, wavy Pre-Raphaelite hair, heavily made-up dark eyes, and a wide, full mouth—that the American public seemed to go for in their more popular women writers. To Judith's way of thinking, she looked about twenty years out of date, preserved in some late-seventies notion of quiescent yet smoldering sexuality circa Stevie Nicks. But she knew enough to know that her taste was not reflective of the population at large.

"Everyone must be thrilled. Steve, especially. I hope you're not letting him hog all the credit."

"I can handle Steve," Roxanne says, smiling.

I'm sure you can, Judith thinks to herself. *Like a dream.*

Dolores sticks her head into the room.

"Sorry I'm late. The dentist kept me longer than expected."

"That's fine," Judith says. "Nothing too serious, I hope."

Her secretary makes a face. "Looks like I'll be needing some root-canal work done."

"Yuck," Roxanne says.

Judith wonders, as a deliberate exercise in self-rejection, what Howard would make of Roxanne's clear-skinned, blue-eyed good looks. But perhaps the question was irrelevant: someone as healthily constituted, emotionally speaking, as Roxanne—someone who embraced the word "cool" and all the bland casualness that went with it—would undoubtedly be immune to Howard Rose's perverse appeal.

"I've got a list of phone messages," Dolores says, "when you're ready."

"I'm out of here," Roxanne says, straightening out the creases on her short linen skirt.

Judith stares at the pile of pink message slips, wondering which calls she might delegate to Dolores and which she can put off till tomorrow. They are all from agents, wanting something from her: an answer on a manuscript that came in minutes ago;

a pub date on a book that isn't even scheduled yet; a higher print run on a small novel that no one but she is excited about and that the agent should have been grateful to her for having the vision and independence of mind to publish in the first place. Then there is yet another editorial letter to get off to the writer who is too lazy to figure out his own book, and more lunches, always more lunches. Everyone wants something from her—everyone, that is, except Howard Rose, who, she noticed with some disappointment, hasn't called her.

"Dolores," she calls out to her secretary. "Give me five minutes, okay?"

Judith closes the door, checks in her leather-bound datebook, and dials his work number. His home number is seared into her brain, almost as though she had been born with it in place, but she almost never calls him at the office.

"May I speak to Howard, please?"

His secretary has a smoothly friendly voice, much like Dolores's.

"May I ask who's calling?"

"Judith," she says, "Judith Stone."

"One minute, please. I'll check to see if he is available."

She can't believe how nervous she feels while she's waiting, her heart is beating fast and she has actual goose bumps on her arms. Will he be his welcoming self? Or his distant, dismissive one? Dr. Jekyll or Mr. Hyde? Maybe she shouldn't have called him at work. He seemed to prefer to be the one to call her during the day.

"Hi," he says, his voice flat verging on annoyed.

"Hi," she says, shy as a faun with this man who's been inside her, seen her splayed in gapingly receptive positions.

"What's up?"

"I shouldn't have called," she says. "I can hear it in your voice."

"Nope," he says.

It was exactly the response she feared.

"Oh, you're busy," she says. "I'll hang up then."

"It's okay. What'd you want?"

"I don't know what I wanted. I just wanted to say hello, I guess."

He doesn't say anything.

"I don't get you," she says.

"What's not to get?"

"Why do you have to sound so unfriendly? 'Nope.' You said 'Nope' when I said I shouldn't have called. Why couldn't you have said, 'It's not the best time. I'll call you back.' Why shouldn't I call you at the office? You make me feel crazy."

Her voice had risen to an unpleasant, panicky pitch. She must get off the phone, forget about this insane-making man, get back to her other self, the one that dealt fairly well with the demands of her job and enjoyed spending time with Celia and Gerald. Sex couldn't be that important, could it? Or the rest of her life that *un*important?

"You're a nut," he says softly.

"You *want* me to be a nut. It makes you feel good, somehow, to reduce me to this."

"I see," he says, as though she's been explaining something

eminently logical to him, how to work her stereo system or where to find the extra set of keys she's hidden in her kitchen. How many weeks has she actually known him? It suddenly seems to her that ordinary chronological time has collapsed, leaving her in this immeasurable state of anxious need, this chronic longing. Judith Stone looks down a long vista at the end of which a man is whispering, *Tell me where it hurts*.

"You don't," she says. "You don't see at all."

"Let's go away together," he says out of the clear blue, as though they were engaged in a completely different conversation.

"When?"

She is owed vacation time, she could take off on short notice if need be. Summer was the slow season in book publishing, anyway; a lot of people took three-day weekends as a matter of course.

"Forever. You and me forever."

"Oh, Howard," she says, both thrilled at the idea and pained in the knowledge that he doesn't mean it, that he's toying with her.

"We'll talk about it tonight. After I fuck your brains out."

"I've got my period," she says.

She menstruates so infrequently that she's always surprised when she finds blood on her underpants. Why else would she feel the urge to announce it, a mundane monthly event that most women felt no need to acknowledge? She envisions his penis gory with her blood, a samurai lover emblazoned with passion.

"It doesn't matter."

"I always thought men minded it, really." And then, plucking a handy detail out of her accumulated religious facts on file, culled from Hebrew school, she adds: "It's against Jewish law to have sexual relations with a woman during her menstrual period, did you know that?"

"Vaguely," he says, sounding impatient. "We can skip it if you prefer."

"No."

"Eight o'clock. My apartment. Sharp."

"Sharp? Why sharp?"

"Just to see if you can do it."

"Do what?"

"Be on time."

"Oh, Howard," she says, "these little tests of yours . . ."

But it was undeniable: she had always had a problem with time, with the nonnegotiability of three o'clock as opposed to three fifteen, the way people who were on time always terrorized you with their own promptness, the way there was no taking into account one's internal rhythms, of making room for a bout of procrastination or an onset of torpor. She supposed her sense of time was hopelessly precarious. Still, he could be understanding instead of censorious, put it down to a forgivable flaw in her makeup.

"You need them," he says. "Your character needs improving. Fixing, you might say."

"I see," she says, thinking that the problem between them was as basic as this, his wanting to "fix" her personality. The truth was that Howard Rose didn't really like her. Yes, he found her intriguing, sometimes. Lusted after her, definitely. But actually like her for who she was, the way Celia or Gerald liked her? Absolutely not. The other truth, she has to admit, was that she wasn't at all clear that she liked him in any recognizable sense. She admires some aspects of him, for sure—his ability to focus, a certain straight-shooting quality—but feels contempt for others: his general attitude of disdain, his lack of curiosity about people, and his dislike of women verging on full-fledged misogyny. Although she was never sure that it wasn't precisely the simmering undertone of hostility between them that made the sex so good.

"Gotta go," he says. "Business beckons."

"Howard," Judith says softly, stalling for more time, more confirmation. "Do you think about me when we're not together?" She had phrased it that way on purpose—with pointed, almost obsequious modesty—the better to wring some droplet of verbal affection out of him.

"I said I have to go. Catch you later."

When she hangs up, it occurs to her—like a buzzer she has failed to notice—that after the first date he has never again offered to pick her up. It is always she who makes her way over to his apartment, where he waits, like a sultan, reclining among the pillows, possessor of her missing piece.

XVII

EARLY IN AUGUST, on a sticky Thursday night, he calls to suggest they go away for the weekend he has been dangling before her for weeks. She is lying on her bed, naked, the air conditioner humming, feeling virtuous because she's eaten sushi for lunch and next to nothing (i.e., a hollowed-out bagel with a slice of low-fat cheese followed by half a plum) for dinner. In the background the McGarrigles are singing in lugubrious harmony about lost love: "Some say a heart is just like a wheel / When you bend it, you can't mend it." She has a whole collection of these singers who specialize in female pining, who sing in a voice husky with regret about their state of permanent heartbreak for what would never be, the man who got away. It's an art form unto itself, this music of the lovelorn. Karla Bonoff. Valerie Carter. Bonnie Raitt. Lucinda Williams. Iris DeMent. The list went on and on; she knew them all. Everyone else grew up and made do with the compromised measures of adulthood except for these women who looked back in longing for what would never be, like teenage girls eternally struck by a starry night and a cute boy at the wheel.

"Whatya doin', Miz Judith?"

His voice on the other end of the phone—the gruffness of it, its lack of inflection—still gives her a start. It's a voice that bounces off the ear, as though utterance itself were a reluctant act of seduction.

"Lying on my bed."

"Watching TV?"

"No."

"Just lying on your bed?"

"Yes. I was staring at the ceiling when you called."

"Where are your hands?"

The sheer provocation of the question—the suggestion that she is engaging in covert, possibly illicit activity—arouses her, and she feels herself go wet.

"By my side."

"Truth?"

"Howard."

Judith rarely masturbated, in spite of having read enough on the subject of masturbation to know that it had been elevated, sometime during the last twenty years, from a mostly unvoiced and somewhat disapproved-of sexual alternative to an important and wondrous female prerogative. She found dildos unappealing, almost ludicrous, in their blatant toylike aspect, and although she has patiently tried to follow the instructions in such bibles of self-pleasuring as *Our Bodies, Ourselves*, she never quite got the hang of it. There was something about the activity

Judith found forlorn beyond all telling: the mere contemplation of it brought visions of old, flappy-skinned men hunched on the edge of their beds in tiny boardinghouse rooms, riding themselves to solitary pleasure.

"God, it was hot today. Shit, what did they do before air-conditioning? I'm surprised they didn't all kill each other in this city . . ."

"Yeah," she murmurs sympathetically. "Thank goodness they invented it in our lifetime."

"I want you," he says, as though this were a natural extension of discussing the pleasures of air-conditioning, "to take your hands and put them on your breasts."

Judith doesn't say anything.

"Are you doing it?"

"Yes."

"How do they feel?"

"Okay. Soft, I guess."

"Your tits," Howard Rose says, "are memorable. Not to overlook those big ripe nipples."

"Thank you," she says, as though she had just been complimented on her penmanship.

"And now," he says, "before we go any further, I want you to put your finger in your cunt. Just the way I do."

Judith liked the word "cunt," if only because it was so much more descriptive than more clinical-sounding terms; a cunt sounded like a cave covered with moss, which is how she envisioned her vagina.

"Howard," Judith says, "is this why you called?"

"I called," he says, "to invite you to go away with me this weekend. This is just a warm-up. Where is your finger?"

"I'm not comfortable doing this," she says.

Long ago, as a little girl, she had liked the feel of her own finger inside her. Her mother claimed she had once been called into Judith's nursery school to discuss her daughter's "precocious" sexuality; "precocious" had turned out to mean that the young Judith liked to sit and masturbate. Dr. Munch had regarded it as a form of "self-soothing," but it is hard—inconceivable—for Judith to envision a time when she felt so uninhibited. It seems like a sunlit patch that has since clouded over, never to reveal its light again.

"You have a juicy cunt," he says. "You should bottle it."

Her finger is inside her grown-up vagina, hidden under its curly beard, no longer the hairless slit of her libidinous nursery school days. Judith still vividly remembers the dismay she felt at the first sign of her pubic hair—those coarse tendrils springing up, unbidden as weeds, dark against the stark white field of her skin.

"How does it feel to you?"

"I don't know. I mean . . ."

"Go with it, babe."

"I'm trying," she says softly.

"Don't try," he commands. "Go with the flow."

And then, quite unexpectedly, she is opened up like a clam, all the silky insides of her exposed. "Oh, I wish I had a river I could skate away on / I wish I had a river so long . . ." Joni Mitchell singing "River" in a plaintive high-pitched voice suddenly pops into her head. Sex was like a river, her cunt was like a river, too. Everything pleasurable led you away . . . but from what? You had to know where you began to know where you were going and where you were eventually coming back to, and Judith has never been sure enough of any of these markers. Never. *Go with the flow*, he said. Easy for him to say. If she went with the flow, she might end up drowning. No wonder she clung to the riverbank, resisting.

"I love your pussy," he says. "It's warm and wet in there."

"Mm," she says, a sound midway between a grunt and a groan.

"Thaaat's it," he says, Herr Director. "Thatsa girl. Save some for me."

Afraid to float out any further, afraid where the current of her desire will take her, she pulls her finger out.

And then, as though he were lying next to her, he says: "Smell your finger. You smell briny, like the sea."

Judith sniffs her finger tentatively. There is, indeed, something reminiscent of the sea. How could she help but succumb to a man so versed in physical intimacy, so intent on guiding her way out, past the big waves? She would drown in Howard Rose, she has always wanted to drown in someone else, she couldn't keep watching from the shore, alone.

"Howard," she says, "I want to tell you something."

"What, baby? That you want me to give you masturbation lessons every night?"

"Howard," she says, "can't you be serious for a minute? I want to tell you something. Something important."

"Get to it. I've got to watch the news."

"Howard," Judith says. "I think I might . . . I don't know . . . I feel . . . I'm not sure . . . like . . . I could be with you." Better to put it in the conditional than as a reality to be dealt with, he might be more receptive to it.

In his silence, the humming of her air conditioner magnifies into an ominous roar.

"Howard?"

"I heard you."

"Does it bother you that I feel this way? I was afraid to say it. But I had to tell you. I probably shouldn't have."

"Probably not," he says.

"Why?"

He says nothing.

"Howard? Why not? Are you secretly married?"

He laughs his distinct Howard Rose laugh, a slightly constrained chortle.

"I'm the wrong guy."

"Why are you the wrong guy? For me? Or for anyone?"

"For you. Too old, for one thing."

"That's just an excuse. You're not too old."

She liked the disparity in their ages—his being more than a decade older than she was: it made her feel he was well out of boyishness, that he had all those years on her in which to deal with whoever she might turn out to be. A child herself, a little girl, for instance, looking for a daddy, a punitive lover of a father. Her own father was a speck, a shadow, burdened by his patients and his woodworking hobby and concerns exclusive of her, an ardent reader of *The New York Times*, given to sudden bursts of temper. When he died, she didn't know whether she would grieve. Or maybe it would be doubly sad, the loss of a loss, the loss of someone she had never known to begin with.

"Too poor, then."

"You're not poor. And money isn't that important."

Could money hold a candle to sex? Diamonds and emeralds were cold, or exuded a heat of a different sort than she needed. She supposed it was possible to get both—money *and* sex, wrapped up in one man—but from her observation, it seemed to Judith that women usually chose between the two. She had chosen Howard Rose. She wanted to marry him, carry his child, make him smile.

"Think of me as a good lay," he says. "Not someone you'd want to spend your life with."

"But I do."

So, that was it: underneath his contempt for others—for her—his greatest contempt was for himself. She understood it too well, for wasn't there something about men who openly craved her that made her contemptuous, made her want to smash them? They could change roles in an instant, Howard Rose and she, she could be the witholding dominatrix and he the eager submissive, swing your partner, do-si-do.

"Don't," he says, simple as that.

Ah, but they are two of a kind; they were both maimed, damaged, giving back as good as they got. Underneath the belittling sadist lurked a belittled masochist. The only detail of his childhood he has shared with her is that his father frequently resorted to his belt. She would prove his value to him, withstand his lapses into cruelty for the larger good of saving them both.

"Whom, may I ask, are you right for?"

"A different kind of chick."

"'Chick.' I didn't think that word was still in use. Do you see other women?"

"Yes."

"So why are we going away together for the weekend? Why don't you take one of your other chicks?"

"Because I want to take you. You and only you."

"Why haven't you ever married any of these other women?"

"I don't want to marry them."

"Howard," she says, "what do you want from me?"

"I want you to suck me off and then I want you to beg me to fuck you. I want you not to think about anything else ever."

Give up on the long view, her experience of sexual pleasure that quickly mutated into drenched romantic vistas ending in a classic portrait of marital devotion: Wasn't that what he was telling her?

"I can't," she says.

"You will."

Is it a promise or a threat? She has lost the ability to tell the difference; she feels like she used to feel when she was blind-folded during long-ago birthday games of Pin the Tail on the Donkey and then spun around and around, left without a sure-fire choice of direction, just the immediate darkness in front of her eyes.

DIGRESSION #4

DON'T WORRY, I'm planning to keep this short. I myself have gotten used to these pauses in the action—these asides to you, The Reader—and would quite miss them if they were suddenly to disappear. In fact, I've begun to think of these parts of the book as a sort of ongoing pajama party, all of us gathered together in one of our respective houses, dressed in nubby flannel nightgowns, nibbling on popcorn, discussing girlish secrets in the dark. I wonder, do teenage girls still have pajama parties or have they gone the way of other innocent pastimes? The world spins at so fast a pace these days that the present is constantly being eclipsed by the future; it's hard to know which of our references irrevocably date us.

As I said, this speculative interlude will be a relatively quick one, although the reasons for that have little to do with formal novelistic intentions and everything to do with contingency: I'm referring to the fact that I got started late today, kept resisting the Call of the Writer, sure and true. For of course you must understand that there is something inherently confounding about taking time off from life to write about life (which is what novelists, at least, purport to do). Real life—by which I mean "life" as it happens off the pages of all books, full of errands and cups of coffee, buses to catch and phone calls to return, children to tend to and new rolls of toilet paper to put in the dispenser—is inherently ungainly, forever resistant to the shaping impulse of art, and always ready to interfere if you give it the least opening. So yes, I got waylaid. And no, I'm not as disciplined as some.

What I wanted to muse about—albeit hastily, given that I have finally brought myself to the keyboard at the virtual end of the day—is the notion of submission itself. Submission as it relates to women in erotic postures, specifically. At what point, for instance, does the normal acquiescence of amorous intent pass over into the realm of the pathological? We have all heard of those cultures where women have their clitorises clipped or their feet bound, the better to serve men. It hardly needs stating that we who reside in the enlightened Western world are used to regarding such rituals as barbaric in the extreme. But what about the less overt manifestations of the implicit disparity in power between men and women as evidenced in our so-called natural practices? Isn't it, arguably, degrading to perform oral sex, to kneel down as before a pontiff and lick at a penis as though it were a scepter? It all translates into power, finally, doesn't it, power actual and perceived?

It was Queen Victoria, I believe, who was said to have counseled her oldest daughter, Vicky, to think of sexual intercourse as a patriotic duty: "Lie back and think of England." Of course, once you start thinking of erotic activity in terms of social responsibility—as essential to the preservation of empire as the taking of high tea or the changing of the guards—everything begins to fall into place.

But those eminent Victorian times to which I just alluded, when gentlemen still went to prostitutes for the baser sexual services (fellatio specifically), are practically prehistory in terms of the present. "The decades since the sixties," Philip Roth observed in *The Dying Animal*, "have done a remarkable job of completing the sexual revolution. This is a generation of astonishing fellators. There's been nothing like them ever before among their class of young women." It puts a strain on one's imaginative faculties even to try to imagine oneself into a time before MTV and suburban malls, when the very utterance of the word "semen" out loud in a Bloomsbury living room in the summer of 1908 could send shock waves across London. That was then, in other words, and the context to which we are trying to address ourselves is now.

Submission—particularly the acknowledgment of the wish to submit—is a particular problem, or so I would like to suggest, for contemporary women who profess to hold themselves in high regard. Intelligent and ambitious women, with carefully evolved late twentieth-century sensibilities: Where do we turn for a taste of willing compliance without stepping completely out of character? "Every woman," Sylvia Plath infamously declaimed in her poem "Daddy," "adores a Fascist, / The boot in the face, the brute / Brute heart of a brute like you." But look what happened to her, poor brute-lover that she was. I'm guessing you know this already, how early one wintry morning, her young children fast asleep, she put out two bottles of milk for their breakfast and then stuck her fevered head in the oven.

Which, you were perhaps wondering, goes to show what? Other than that Sylvia Plath was inconsolable, albeit gifted, in her fury? What, exactly, you were further wondering (if you haven't wandered off by this point to check out the contents of your refrigerator, looking for something more directly sustaining than what I can provide: an apple, that little wedge of chocolate cake left over from the weekend, some cold macaroni with ketchup that your daughter didn't finish and which you covered with Saran Wrap because you didn't want to throw it out), am I trying to prove? I don't know, it's been a bad day, what can I say. I suppose I mean that sanity is some sort of check against a too-radical embrace of the submissive element in one's own makeup. And lest you think in your blithe way that you've escaped, remember that there are many ways to imprison yourself with the object of your desire, so many other kinds of subjugation besides the man-on-top, "lie back and think of England" variety:

(1) You can phone said object of desire and say nothing when he picks up, hoping your silence will be interpreted correctly and responded to; (2) you can hang up millions of times on his answering machine; (3) you can have obsessive and time-consuming conversations with friends as to the exact nature and hope(less)(ful)ness of your passion; (4) you can compose love letters—or emails—in which you twirl around in all

your well-phrased charms; (5) you can sit in coffee shops, staring into space, conducting romantic crescendos in your head. I've always thought women are more inclined than men to such busywork in the name of love—the effluvia of erotic servitude, you might call it—but then again how well I, for one, know men is anyone's guess. And now, ladies and gentlemen, as a token of my gratitude to you for sticking by me while I meander my way back to the story, please accept these, the further entangled adventures of Howard Rose and Judith Stone.

XVIII

THEY WERE PLANNING to leave the city in the early evening, which meant that she had to get up excruciatingly early Friday morning to pack before she left for work. Packing was a hurdle for Judith, had always been. She would have liked to travel with fifty-some-odd pieces of matching luggage, the way Marlene Dietrich and the Duchess of Windsor used to travel. She remembered reading somewhere that Jackie Kennedy and her sister, Lee Radziwill, had traveled to India with eighty-four pieces of luggage between them. But no one traveled that way anymore, not even movie stars. The contemporary mode was to pack light, and Judith had no idea how to pack light. The whole issue of what to take, what to leave home, how much was too much, seemed to evoke—albeit on a small scale—the general, larger dilemma of her life. To wit: Who was she? Or, to put it another way: Who was she trying to be on any given occasion? And which accessory—shoe, scarf, bag, earrings, what have you—would best demonstrate the fluid, un-pin-down-able persona she was, however briefly and transitorily, trying on? If you didn't know who you were, you needed enough changes of clothing to carry you through a whole range of selves.

And what if she were to be hit by a car while she was away, or had her head smashed by a falling tree, never to return home to her apartment with all its things squirreled away in drawers and closets? There was always the chance that you would die when you went away, even for the weekend: she needed lots of her possessions with her, lest she drop dead. Of course, even Judith recognizes that this obsessively morbid view of each and every departure failed to take into account the fact that she wouldn't need an extra set of underwear or a second nightgown if her life were to come to an abrupt end.

Celia was a whiz at helping her pack; Judith's affection for her friend overflowed at those times when Celia came over and, pad and pen in hand, made a succinct list of the items Judith would need on a particular business trip or vacation. Celia understood her anxieties enough to allow for an extra pair of shoes or a beloved but unwieldy bottle of shampoo, yet managed to steer Judith clear of her tendency to cart her entire bathroom cabinet with her. But she can hardly call on Celia at five thirty in the morning, so she is left to her own devices. The forecast called for god-awful weather—humid and overcast, with a chance of showers. What should she wear to an inn somewhere in Rhinebeck with a man who, aside from in bed, she doesn't know all that well?

In the three months since she had first met Howard Rose they had gone out to dinner a couple of times and to the movies five, maybe six times. He had made dinner for her twice, which consisted of his warming up some pre-seasoned hamburgers and doctoring rotisserie chicken, but she was touched by even these minimal gestures. Just as she was touched by the few items of clothing he kept in a bedside drawer in her apartment, several pairs of socks and some changes of underwear. He also hung a white and a blue shirt in her closet together with a pair of chinos. These things made him feel real to her, someone who existed outside of her thoughts. But so far they hadn't actually done all that much together in the way of the outside world; they weren't a concert- or operagoing sort of couple, and she hadn't ventured to introduce him to Celia or Gerald. Mostly they talked on the phone. And engaged each other sexually.

There was a certain strain in going away with a man, no doubt about it; there was always the possibility of romance palling, of running out of things to say to each other, of discovering that two days together was more than enough. Sometimes it seemed to Judith that all the problems of her life would be solved in one fell blow if she were to hanker after her own sex. Did lesbians, like her college friend Mindy, get anxious about what to pack—about how they'd look to their beloved lolling poolside—when they went away together?

And then there was always, at least for her, the Bathroom Problem. She had begun to discuss it with Dr. Munch, way back before she had met Howard Rose and there wasn't an actual man in whose eyes she wanted to seem perpetually sweet-smelling. It didn't lend itself to easy resolution, this body-which-fucks and body-which-defecates split. Was she the only one who suffered from the problem of extreme discomfort over the reality—the stink—of her own excrement? As for other people's, there is nothing she finds more mortifying than going into a public toilet after someone else had just gotten done befouling it: it makes her want to separate herself from the rest of defecating humankind.

At least in earlier times, before the invention of air fresheners and room deodorizers and scented candles and all the other gizmos of olfactory subterfuge, they were honest about the conflict. Weren't those dramatists of the sixteenth and seventeenth centuries obsessed with the odor of decomposing flesh underneath the fair-skinned maiden, the skull rattling across the stage? And look at the eighteenth century's Jonathan Swift, the famed and scholarly author of *Gulliver's Travels*, for a case of mind over odiferous matter. In a poem about a lover's discovery of his mistress Celia's chamberpot, published in 1732, he wrote: "Oh! Celia, Celia, Celia shits!" Yes, that was the word he used, precisely and scandalously and centuries ahead of himself. Of course, this allusion to the malodorous reality that lies behind the "sweet and cleanly" Celia was probably seen as a bit odd, then as now, a portent of Swift's eventual decline into madness.

They were, when you came right down to it, the two great unfairnesses of living in the late twentieth century: the burden of intimate deception, of pretending that your shit smelled like a bouquet, and the burden of packing light.

At precisely five thirty, Howard Rose picks her up in front of her office building in a rented white Volvo. Judith drags her overstuffed and monumentally heavy piece of luggage from the curb and hurls it into the back seat of the car before stepping into the seat next to him. She notes with a degree of unanticipated irritation that he has neither moved to open the door for her nor offered to help with the luggage. Perhaps because she is going away with him for the first time, she feels newly conscious of—even alarmed by—his lack of civility. In bed it had a certain charm, the way he proceeded without benefit of social graces, but on a sticky Friday evening in August, feeling weary before they have even begun the two-hour trip, her eyes scratchy from lack of sleep, she suddenly finds herself longing for a different, kinder man. Was there any hope of changing him? Or was their relationship founded on the principle of her accommodation to his ways?

"Would you like me to stop for a coffee?"

"That would be nice," she says, surprised by the offer.

"You're wearing a skirt," he observes, maneuvering his way expertly through traffic. "How come?"

"I don't know," she says. "I was in the mood."

"You dumb fuck," he says, suddenly slamming down on the brakes as a car comes up from behind and practically sideswipes them.

She picked the skirt, a long flowered one with slits up the sides, deliberately this morning, the better to feature her legs. Looking straight ahead at the road, with one hand on the wheel,

Howard slides his other hand up her slit. She becomes instantly wet and lets her legs fall to either side.

"I see," he says, then puts his hand back on the wheel.

"What do you see?"

"You," he says.

"What about the rest of me?" she asks. "The part that has nothing to do with this?"

"With what?"

"With sex. With getting aroused. There's got to be more to you and me than sex."

Didn't he claim in that very first phone call to admire her mind, which he appeared to have absolutely minimal interest in? It has occurred to her more and more of late how little they talk about—his cases, from time to time, and once in a while she'll mention a book she's editing. But a lot of their time together passes in relative silence. They have made a stop for coffee and now the radio is playing, some kind of classic rock station, the Rolling Stones snarling "Jumpin' Jack Flash." Howard doesn't say anything and Judith looks out the window at the Hudson River, which glimmers in the setting sun as though it is on fire. She closes her eyes and leans back against her seat.

"Tired?" he asks.

"Yeah, I didn't get much sleep last night."

"Rest your weary head, my love," he says.

She thinks of the Auden lines—"Lay your sleeping head, my love / Human on my faithless arm"—and almost mentions it, then thinks better of it. She loved Auden's poetry and had studied his influence on Philip Larkin (her all-time favorite, despite the fact that one of her professors had told her she was too young to like Larkin) and other postwar British poets. She wondered again—it was a frequent regret of hers—why she had left graduate school, with its discussion of unreliable narrators and perforated texts. She could be reading for a living now, composing learned papers on writers she loved, instead of foisting *Misty's Children* on an unsuspecting public. She wonders whether other people think of their lives in so wistful a fashion—as a series of smaller and larger regrets—and then she falls asleep somewhere along the way, her head sliding toward Howard's shoulder. She wakes up once when he stops the car somewhere in the middle of nowhere to fill up on gas only to fall asleep again. He shakes her gently when they pull up in front of the inn.

"We're here," he says.

She has been dreaming about summer camp, about a boy she had a crush on who gave her her first French kiss.

The inn strikes her as somewhere between ramshackle and charming, and for a minute she wonders how Howard found it. The man at the front desk seems muted, barely able to crack a welcome smile, and Judith wonders whether he has Asperger's or is on some kind of sedating medication. She asks if there's a ladies' room near the lobby, and early in the morning she will come down the stairs in the dark to make use of it. Their room is small, with a lumpy four-poster bed and a rocking chair. The wallpaper is a faded print and there is a braided oval rug on the floor. The bathroom is minuscule, equipped with mingy toiletries—two wrapped itty-bitty bars of soap and tiny bottles of generic shampoo and conditioner—and the plastic shower stall is practically on top of the toilet. For a moment she fights off a feeling of panic, or perhaps it is claustrophobia: What is she doing hours from the city with a man she has become addicted to but doesn't quite trust? The bathroom puts her in mind of Hitchcock's *Psycho* and she briefly considers the possibility that Howard is a genuine psychopath who will stab her to death while she is taking a shower. There is nowhere to go, she realizes with a knot of anxiety, should she need to get away. At home she can leave his apartment but now she is stuck with him.

"What's the matter?" he asks. He has stripped down to his underwear and is about to take a shower.

"Nothing," she says.

"Not swanky enough for you?"

"What?"

"The place?"

"It's . . . cozy."

"You really think so?"

"I do."

"Granted," he says, "it's a little on the cramped side."

She laughs, grateful that they share a similar view of their surroundings.

The sheets on the bed are worn through, the way she likes them, and for a while they lie side by side reading, in a way they rarely do in the city. She is skimming a manuscript set in Georgia, about a family of lovable eccentrics whose antic doings she has tired of halfway through, and he is reading a recently published biography of Churchill.

"Do you like biographies? I've never seen you read fiction," Judith says.

"There's nothing to learn from novels," he answers obtusely. "They're all made-up, nothing you can prove." She wanted to say that was exactly the point of novels, but decided not to take him on.

"I love Churchill," she says. "Think where we Jews would be without him."

"True," he says. "He made mistakes but he's a pretty heroic figure when all is said and done." He doesn't seem inclined to talk any more. So Judith puts on a robe—a silky floral affair she had thrown into her suitcase at the last minute—and ventures into the bathroom, which now strikes her as nothing less than ominous. She bangs up against the tight contours of the shower stall as she washes herself, then powders herself and sprays on some perfume that smells of lilac. She puts on a demure cotton nightgown—so demure that she could be the virginal love interest in some 1950s western—and slips into bed next to a naked Howard. At some point he turns off his reading light and leans over, kissing her on the neck, a long, lover-like kiss. She turns toward him and studies his face in the low beam of her reading light: the lean hollows of his cheeks, his close-cropped beard, and his eyes, suggestive of a vulnerability he doesn't otherwise reveal. As though in keeping with this small shift in him—or in how she views him—Howard takes her in his arms almost solemnly, no longer playing at being the ever-elusive partner to her wishful yet determined pursuit of him. Their sex is closer to actual lovemaking than it's ever been and they snuggle afterward—he has always been a snuggler, despite its seeming a departure from his usual style—his arm holding her close to him.

For a moment Judith wonders whether the tide has turned, whether they are meant to be a devoted, hand-in-hand couple after all—a glossy, picture-perfect postcard of togetherness: *Greetings from us!* It should make her happy, but something about the image makes her uneasy.

The next morning she wakes up late to discover that Howard has already left the room and gone downstairs for breakfast, leaving behind the smoky, slightly cloying scent of Old Spice. She gets dressed quickly in a sweatshirt and jeans and decides to forgo any makeup—the little improving touches she usually bothers with, lining her eyes and then swiping them with mascara, putting on blush—in favor of her ungarnished face. Howard is sitting at a small table by the window in the breakfast room, which looks out on the full green trees of summer, eating scrambled eggs and reading the Metro section of the *Times*. He is wearing small, very dark, pimp-like sunglasses that for a moment put her in mind of *The Graduate*, a movie that she thought of as talismanic in the vision it offered of romantic pursuit.

It has always been one of her favorite scenes: the first date between Benjamin Braddock (Dustin Hoffman) and Elaine Robinson (Katharine Ross), whom he is dead set on alienating, having been sleeping with her mother and warned off the daughter.

Benjamin roars along in his red Alfa Romeo, ignoring Elaine's attempts at conversation, and takes her to a strip joint where he sits at a front table and ogles a stripper with impressive breasts who circles the tassels on her nipples over Elaine's head, reducing her to silent, unsniffling tears. Finally Elaine races out sobbing, saying "I want to go home," and a stricken Benjamin runs after her. When he catches up with her, he turns her face toward him and gives her a long, passionate kiss. Hostility melting into ardor: Why did this progression excite Judith so, make it seem worth her while, rather than the one of sustained affection blossoming into love? There was something in her that couldn't respond to more ordinary scenarios—or was it more tender expressions?—of intimacy. They left her no place to hide, would show her up as a woman deeply, ludicrously in love. She wonders again whether Howard feels any real love for her under the incessant drama, the push-pull of their sexual entwinement.

"Good morning," she says, trying for civility.

He looks up at her over the paper but doesn't respond. Judith pauses to order orange juice, coffee, and French toast from an eager young waiter with a shock of blond hair he keeps pushing out of his eyes. His sweetness, set off against Howard's coldness, suddenly makes her feel sad. Should she cry like the doll-like Elaine, tears sliding soundlessly from big hazel eyes, made even bigger by a fringe of false lashes? Would Howard feel contrite like Benjamin? It didn't seem likely.

"What's bothering you?" she asks.

She knows he's capable of sitting through a meal in silence if he is angered or irritated, but she has never been comfortable with this kind of radical withdrawal, this cutoff of all communication. It reminded her too much of her mother, who would set her mouth grimly and stop speaking to Judith for days at a time after a quarrel.

"You. You bother me."

"Why?"

She feels a familiar wave of despair overcome her, a sense that she is about to be abandoned by the roadside.

"You're inconsiderate," he says, biting his words off. "Your Highness kept me waiting in this fucking place for almost an hour until she was ready to put in an appearance."

"What are you talking about, Howard? I was *asleep*."

He says nothing and goes back to reading the paper, neatly folded into quarters the way she never manages to do. She watches him, the deliberate way he drinks his coffee and bites into a slice of toast, and suddenly feels a surge of blind rage rise in her—the sort of rage she has always been capable of but has been afraid to expose Howard to. What had happened to their genuine closeness of the night before, her dreams of transforming him through the power of love? She feels like slapping him across the face, if only to disturb his imperturbability.

"You know what?"

He doesn't answer her.

"You're a jerk. A fucking jerk. A pathetic little man who gets off on treating women like shit. Underneath it all I think you hate women." She says it like she means it, almost shouting, prodding herself forward. He stares neutrally at her and says nothing.

"I don't know what I'm doing with you," Judith continues. "I feel sorry for you. You and your 'Do I own you now?' crap. No, you didn't, you don't, you never will. Why don't you stick with your criminals, those perverted assholes you defend? You're as sick as any of them."

She puts her napkin down and waits for him to do something, fall abjectly to his knees in the face of her tirade, beg her forgiveness. Instead he scribbles something on a napkin and pushes it toward her. She reads his message, printed in crooked block letters, like a child's: "I don't love you anymore."

She suddenly feels deflated, like a pricked balloon, her anger fled, replaced by a feeling of abjection at having gone too far. Still, even if she were inclined to try to make amends, a part of her knows he would only disdain her the more for backing down and making conciliatory noises.

For the rest of the day, Judith entertains herself, taking solitary walks, trying to catch some rays under a mostly cloudy sky on the patio, and, as the afternoon wanes, reading on one of the sagging couches in the parlor next to the breakfast room. She asks the friendly woman at the front desk for a train schedule and books herself a ticket and taxi for a six-thirty departure from Rhinecliff. She has no idea where Howard has gone, not even when she goes upstairs to pack her bag; she doesn't see his car in the parking lot and for all she knows, he has left, driven home. She admires herself for acting with conviction for once, even if feigned, even as she wonders how long she'll be able to stand her life without him. After all, try as she might, she has never been good at follow-through.

XIX

"DEAR HOWARD," she types on her old warhorse of a typewriter, the military-gray IBM Selectric on which she still composes drafts of letters and memos, which Dolores then recasts perfectly on the computer that takes up half her desk. "I think about you all the time."

It is seven thirty on a Tuesday night at the beginning of September. Judith and Howard haven't talked since their disastrous weekend away, which has effectively reduced her to a state of anxiety mixed with longing, leading to endless repetitive phone calls explaining Howard's hold on her to an increasingly impatient Celia. Against her better judgment, she practically jumps every time the phone rings at night, hoping it is him. She has spent the last two weekends of August sleeping on a couch in the living room at Celia's group rental in Westhampton and in between moping and reading manuscripts has acquired a deep tan. She has also lost her appetite and dropped a few pounds, with the result that her cheekbones look more pronounced than ever. All of it seems a waste without Howard to admire her. As she types, she keeps noticing the contrast between her sun-browned hands and her fingernails, polished in her usual shade of palest pink. Judith has always liked that about a tan—the way it makes everything that isn't tanned stand out and look better by contrast: the whites of her eyes, her teeth, and her nails. She leans back in her chair, surveys her handiwork, then x's out "all the time" and types in "constantly." Yes, better: "I think about you constantly."

"I know"—she goes on tapping away at the keyboard, thinking she'd better keep this short or she'll die of asphyxiation: the air-conditioning had been turned off a half hour earlier by some preset central control—"I've said some terrible things to you, and that all we seem to be doing is fighting of late. I probably meant it when I said that you hated women at heart. Or at least me. And that I thought you liked representing criminals—'bad guys' as you call them—because they make you seem like a good guy, which would be difficult to put over otherwise."

Judith is beginning to feel clammy in her airless office. How long, she wonders, does it take for the supply of oxygen to run out in a sealed space? (This is the kind of question she'd be able to answer had she paid closer attention in science class, instead of doodling in her notebook.) And what—she continues talking to herself—was the whole point of writing this letter to try to reingratiate herself with Howard, to get him to penetrate her again, if she merely repeated on paper all the accusations of gross personality disturbance that she had made in person?

Then again, didn't everyone, from the women's magazines

and self-help books to her friend Celia, claim that men required flattery almost as their due? It seems strange to Judith that feminism could talk itself blue in the face and still women around the world continued to take upon themselves the burdensome role of elected coddlers and soothers of the tender male ego. As though the need for dewy-eyed confirmation were gender-specific! She, for one, could have used a daily dose of buttering up as much as any man; her ego smarted to the touch, as anyone who knew her well could vouch for.

Still, it was getting her nowhere, this internal one-woman rebellion—unless she planned to take up lesbianism. It certainly was getting her nowhere with Howard Rose, who, under his rough-and-ready act, clearly required more sweet talk than most. Here, then, was the opportunity to point out his charms; to describe the spell he cast on her and her willingness to fulfill his every whim, concubine-like. She'd approach him the way you'd approach a frisky colt, that's what she'd do: stroke him, feed him sugar cubes, *flatter him.*

"But I also mean other things," Judith goes on typing: "I mean it, for instance, when I say I love you. And that I want to darn your socks for you. And that I'll learn how to bake cheesecake for you the way you like it, creamy and lemony. And get you to smile that infrequent, boyish smile of yours. Come back, Howard. I promise to bend over so you can contemplate my ass as much as you like. I miss you and want you to call me so I can come rushing over to your apartment and you can ask me if you own me after you enter me with that . . ."

Here Judith pauses for a moment to reflect, the hum of the

typewriter the only sound to break the silence of the office. She has to watch out that in her new determination to gush like a geisha she doesn't get carried away and end up sounding like bad Henry Miller. Or, worse yet, the Letters column in *Penthouse*, which Howard subscribed to. ". . . after you enter me with that . . ." That what? What can she call his penis that would differentiate it from the generic article? She wants a term that would indicate how much it meant to her, personally. Every man had a penis, it was standard male equipment, but few of them had a penis like Howard Rose's, she is convinced of it. It was, in the end, his penis she longed for—or, at least the way he used it—building up to the moment of insertion and then the way it felt inside her. That, and his sudden, unexpected leaps into softness, even intimacy. Howard Rose's moments of sweetness were all the more precious because they were at such odds with the caustic armor he encased himself in most of the time: it was like catching a glimpse of a submerged continent—some wonderful, light-filled place out of a fairy tale.

These moments, when he wrapped his arms around her and snuggled against her; or when he listened with genuine interest to one of her complicated emotional dramas and offered dry but surprisingly perceptive comments; these moments, put together with his penis—stick, that was what he called it, self-mockingly, now it came to her. "Stick" or, alternately, "rod." Whatever the name, there was something magical about it, almost Lawrentian. She returns to where she has left off. ". . . enter me with that nice big stick of yours. I want you to own me, do you know that? Maybe that's why I'm so difficult. Forgive me, sweet warrior prince."

Judith sits back in her rolling executive desk chair, pleased with herself. "Sweet warrior prince," he'll like that one. And the cheesecake reference, that will endear her to him, too. Although she really should learn how to bake, it was a skill that would serve her in life, with or without Howard Rose. She had considered delivering a cheesecake (store-bought, but they were so homemade-tasting these days he'd be none the wiser) to his apartment the day after they had stopped talking but it felt too pathetic even to her. Earlier on, when they had fought, she had been capable of such gestures, like ordering an arrangement of flowers to be sent to him, with a short dramatic note attached, its message filched word for word from one of her favorite love-demented songs, "Heart Like a Wheel": "My love for you," she had scribbled on the tiny white card provided by the florist, "is like a sinking ship and my heart is on that ship out in mid-ocean." No greeting, no sign-off, just the stark desperation of the words themselves, sputtering like a Roman candle. She had stuffed the card in its tiny white envelope, where it would eventually make its way, pinned near the top of the bouquet, to Howard Rose.

(Already then, Celia had thought she was crazy: "Isn't *he* the one supposed to be sending *you* flowers? Why are you so stuck on this nutjob, anyway? You send him flowers and then he majestically agrees to see you again to abuse you some more. Judith, when are you going to work these things out in their proper setting? With a shrink instead of with some sexual deviant who is thirteen years older than you and has never gotten it together to marry, because he's been too busy perfecting the art of torturing women like you!") But four months into knowing Howard Rose she feels too tentative—too unhinged by the gusts of their relationship—to leave herself wide open with such displays of adoration. The letter will have to do.

There is one more problem: How should she sign it? He called her "Jew-woman" sometimes, which he considered enormously funny; other times he called her "SJW," an acronym from the personals column signifying that a single Jewish woman had placed the ad. (She read the personals in the back of various publications with great attention, but had never actually tried meeting a man that way. In any case, there were always many more women placing ads than men, as if men were a disappearing breed. She wondered if Howard Rose did more than read them.) "Hello, Jew-woman," he would say when she picked up the phone. Or a message on her answering machine: "Rose here. Howard Rose. How's my SJW doing today?" The only times he referred to her by her given name were when they were in bed—as though it was only under the sheets, without their clothes on, that she became real to him. She felt her body clutch up at the memory of his slowly, deliberately fucking her, reaching behind to put a finger in her anus, filling her up at both ends, relieving her of the burden of being alone in her skin, his tongue in her mouth, his kisses flirty rather than sloppy.

In the hot little cell of her office, the Jew-woman in love with a deviate absently scratches a mosquito bite on her left leg with her right, sandaled foot and takes a pen from the pencil holder (an antiquey-looking thing she had hauled back from a trip to London to meet with British agents) on her desk. "Love," she writes in her scratchy, uncurvy handwriting, "Judith (aka Jewwoman)." There, she'd covered all the angles; no one could accuse her of a lack of irony but she had also come out into the open, undisguised by the ribald code (or was it merely disdainful? Celia, undoubtedly, would find nothing affectionate about his pet names for her) of their relationship. The deed was done.

Judith turns off the lights and then stands in her office doorway, looking out on the empty hallway and the lineup of closed doors. For a moment she entertains the thought of causing mayhem to the organization of which she is a part—scattering books all over the floor, marking up the walls, and overturning all the neat, clean-surfaced desks. She could just envision how they'd all react: Cal would hide out till the hurricane had passed, take an extra-long lunch, and then go home early to catch up on some manuscripts; Steve would stomp around in one of his white rages, his thin upper lip momentarily disappeared into the furious set of his mouth; Katrina would be on the phone instantly, bearing the grim details to her well-placed cronies— implying, as she stroked her neck thoughtfully, that the violation she was describing had to do with some larger horror within her adoptive culture itself. It would be left to the various assistants, with Dolores solicitously at the helm, to set the place to rights.

No one would be any the wiser; they'd think some afterhours caretaker had gone berserk—a security guard, say, or one of the cleaning women who came in promptly at six o'clock to pass a desultory vacuum cleaner over the floor and to empty the wastebaskets of their plastic liners. At the end, everyone would come around to Katrina's elegant little theory: it would be put down to the rage born of too little pay and too much drudgery on the part of someone who was too tired—too disadvantaged, really—to read any of the books her company published, commercial or literary. No one would think of ascribing it to her, Judith Stone, up-and-coming editor, never at a loss for words, her hair always washed. Sure, she was taken for a bit of an eccentric, but no one had grounds to suspect her of the angry fantasies that festered in her heart.

Really, she was going batty with unsatisfied desire. Or was it grief that was unbalancing her? Was it all Howard Rose, in other words, or had this capacity always lurked within her—some vast sadness waiting to cast its pall over her? Drenched in sweat from the lack of ventilation, Judith continues to stand in the doorway, as if she were waiting for a signal. She has the letter in her hand, ready to put into the outgoing mail tray. A lot of good it would do. He'd call her again, make love to her again, because he liked playing with her, testing her limits. She could see it—saw it, clear as day, from the moment she had met him. She didn't need the ever-loyal Celia or anyone else to see it for her.

Judith Stone shuts the door firmly behind her. It is a quarter past eight. She has to be back on these very premises so soon that she might as well set up camp for the night and surprise everyone by being at her desk uncharacteristically early. Ugh. She wants a new life, that's what she wants. Meanwhile, there is still the supermarket to stop at before she goes home; she needs paper towels and something to put in her refrigerator to see her through the week. Cereal, and milk, she remembers scribbling those down, and there were some other items as well. She had made a list that morning before she left the house but she feels too worn out to try to locate it within the depths of her bag. On her way out of the building she pauses to sign out at the desk. As she smiles wearily at the guard, it comes to her in a burst of clarity why she has never been a natural reader of mysteries: she was so busy consulting with her emotions that she always overlooked the obvious clues. Of course they'd figure out who had trashed the office: they had only to look under their noses— check the sign-out book or talk with the guard—to find out that she, Judith Stone, had been the last to leave the scene of the crime.

XX

"I'M TENSE," Gerald says.

"Don't be tense," Judith says.

"I don't know if this is a good idea."

"Don't be silly," Judith says.

The two of them are walking up Fifth Avenue on their way to her sister's apartment for dinner. It is a Friday night in November, and Judith is startled to see that the trees in Central Park are nearly bare, in readiness for winter. She remembers when time used to pass too slowly, when it seemed like the days of a month were as long as her whole life. That had been true throughout her childhood and even into her twenties. When had it changed, so that the temperature caught her unawares, and she shivered in too light a jacket? Now she couldn't keep track of one season before the next one was upon her.

"Can you tell me why we're doing this again?" Gerald asks. "Was it my idea or yours?"

Judith links her arm in his as they enter the building. Inside is a gleaming lobby, intimately lit by wall sconces, attended by what seems like a horde of doormen.

"I thought you might find it interesting, sociologically speaking: Jews at their ritual Sabbath dinner. The food should be good, and their apartment's pretty amazing."

Judith's brother-in-law, Elliot Dubin, was rich when Rebecca married him (rich enough to buy a large apartment and then proceed with visionary zeal to gut and rebuild it from scratch) and seemed to amass more wealth with every passing year. The Dubins were in real estate—"property," as John Galsworthy would have called it, if it had been nineteenth-century England instead of twentieth-century America, and if Elliot's family had been other than Jewish. They owned office buildings in Manhattan and shabby apartment houses off in the other boroughs, away from scrutiny. From Judith's vantage point the real-estate business seemed to be a kind of Mount Olympus of money, affording ever-higher summits to be scaled. Recently Rebecca and her husband had put a wine cellar in their summer house and enlarged the heated, intricately shaped pool, set among an abundance of flowering shrubs. Judith could see herself making selective use of the affluent props of her sister's life—the shimmering gray-blue of the pool a perfect backdrop for her relentless pursuit of Howard Rose.

"Do they know I'm gay?" Gerald asked in the elevator, as it ascended soundlessly toward the seventh floor. Judith has noticed that the fancier the building the more hushed its inner workings, elevator gears and buzzers and such. If it was true that money didn't buy happiness—which she wasn't convinced of, in any case—it certainly seemed to buy quiet.

"Gerald, you hardly want *me* to know you're gay. For the longest time I was supposed to pretend I didn't know, much less talk about it. Remember? Of course I haven't mentioned it."

The elevator door opens on a small hallway, papered in a grayish-green stripe. A tall arrangement of flowers in soft tones stands in a vase on a Frenchy-looking table, above which hangs a round mirror in a gilded frame that, in turn, reflects the flowers. The whole effect is one of restrained opulence—the wish to make a statement vying with the impulse to let things speak for themselves. Money, Judith couldn't help but notice, came with conflicts all its own, nuances of taste that seemed beside the point if you didn't have it to begin with.

"Pish-posh," Gerald says.

"I told you," Judith says. "Are you ready?"

Gerald straightens his tie in front of the mirror and salutes.

"Aye, aye."

After having drinks in the living room, which features Elliot's prized collection of American art—Arthur Dove, Charles Sheeler, Marsden Hartley, and a lilac-tinged Richard Diebenkorn that Judith covets—the assembled group proceeds to the dining room. At the table it is Gerald who seems at ease—regaling everyone with publishing stories, making the buying and selling of books sound positively exotic—and Judith who feels nervous. Why, indeed, has she come here tonight, bringing Gerald along as a frisky mascot? She is aware of different worlds clashing together inside of her like cymbals, making a loud, discordant noise. She wonders what the other guests, two couples from the synagogue her sister and brother-in-law have recently joined, make of them: Did they see Gerald and her as emissaries from some wild and crazy planet where you lived on air, throwing money at grateful authors, co-ops and private schools be damned? Are they wondering who she is to Gerald and he to her; who she is, period?

"What a beautiful Shabbat you've made," one of the women says to Rebecca. Judith has trouble keeping the two wives apart: they are both painfully thin and dressed in similarly tailored dresses with gold buttons.

"We think it's important to show the next generation," Elliot says, speaking between spoonfuls of fruit salad, which has been served for dessert along with bittersweet chocolate cookies in the shape of leaves. "Give them a sense of belonging."

"I don't know, honey," Judith's sister says. "That sounds so formal and thought-out. Besides which, at three and a half Charlie's still too young to belong anywhere, don't you think? I think we did it more for us, really."

In the last year Elliot has turned to Judaism with the same entrepreneurial gusto he applies to other aspects of his life. First you make a lot of money, Judith thinks to herself, biting into a cookie, then you repent. She has never noticed the lack of religion in her sister and brother-in-law's lives before they started importing it, but then again she had never noticed the other absences they deemed it necessary to fill.

"You're right, darling," Elliot says. "What I'm really saying,

I guess, is that religious ritual serves as a useful organizing principle. Like marriage, or any other convention the world agrees to abide by."

"Sounds deadly," Judith mutters to no one.

"Really, Elliot," one of the dark-haired women is saying, "you make it sound so joyless. So passionless."

"But marriage isn't really about passion, Leslie, is it," Rebecca protests, surprising Judith, who has been in the habit of thinking of her sister as an unconflicted advocate of connubial life and its pleasures. Whereas Judith herself always looked upon married life as a grand hoax committed by the coupled upon the uncoupled: look what we've pulled off, with no one bothering to admit that domesticity and erotic intrigue didn't cohabit particularly well. How sustainable was sexual desire at close quarters, anyway? How much could you be turned on by someone whose hair you had to scoop out of the shower drain or who had left the toothpaste drying on the counter with the top off? No wonder her sister and brother-in-law had opted for separate bathrooms.

Judith guessed that maybe men told the truth to each other; that explained why they were always off together, leering and ogling as they sat in bars, or spilling the beans in their locker rooms. But if women voiced their doubts, the whole world would come to a stop; the human race would literally die out. In her heart of hearts she thought of marriage and pregnancy as conspiracies perpetuated by women against their own kind, generation after generation, ensnaring you from birth until there was no way out and you were already standing under the chuppah, or pushing a baby out between gasps of pain.

"I've never believed in marriage, myself," one of the sleek-looking husbands is saying, "but look where that's gotten me."

"Sweetheart," his wife says, the prettier of the two women, "don't tell me you're not happy."

"Of course I'm happy," he says, winking broadly in Judith's direction. "I've done it twice, haven't I? Would a man willingly enter the prison gates a second time if he hadn't been happy there the first time around?"

And now Elliot is asking Gerald a question that makes him flush, about his own romantic history. Do they suspect? Or do they have intimations? Should she help them all out, explain that Gerald is different from them? That he likes the taste of men's cum in his throat? And how have they gotten onto this subject, anyway? If she's not careful she'll be called upon next, to run an X-rated film of her blatantly self-destructive affair with Howard Rose, nothing left to the imagination and not a wedding bell pealing anywhere.

"I want Gerald to marry *me*," Judith says with what she hopes is a lighthearted air.

The whole table is silent for a moment, as though she's just whipped off all her clothes and revealed herself to be a transvestite.

"News to me," Gerald says. "But I'll consider it."

"Let's sing," Rebecca says. "Some Shabbat songs."

"Good idea," Leslie says brightly. "Some *zemirot*."

Elliot begins to sing in his strong, rather melodious voice, his Sunday-school grasp of Hebrew buoyed by a year's worth of private lessons with an Israeli tutor. There was something so propelled—so forward-march—about her brother-in-law that was really quite admirable. Judith wonders, as she listens to him tackle the *Shir Ha-Ma'alot*, how such a personality style might translate into the bedroom. It was no doubt shortsighted of her to think that only bent personalities made for dashing sexual companions. She looks over at her sister, whose belly is swelled with the next Dubin heir; it was clear her sister and brother-in-law came together for procreative purposes, if nothing else: first came love, then came marriage, then came Charlie and his sibling-to-be in the baby carriage. A nice orderly progression, and if one or two phases didn't quite match up, it was the general impression that counted in the long run. Of course sex for procreative purposes was one thing, sex for its own sake another: she couldn't imagine Elliot and Rebecca doing the things she'd done . . .

She'd never bring the four of them together, that's for sure: the very thought of it made her shudder. God knows what her sister and brother-in-law would make of Howard Rose in all his insouciant, unrepentant splendor. They'd write him off as a bad bet in a second. As for Howard, he would look down his nose at the very idea of an Elliot, would find him too conventional by half, deem him to be the sort of man too busy acquiring ever-greater swaths of the world to realize there were easier ways of asserting one's power—that there were women out there to own, women like Judith with their guard down, no dinner guests, no conventions the world agreed to abide by, between the sheets, wet and ready.

"Do come again," Rebecca says by the door. Her perfume

wafts out deliciously, something not too sweet yet stirring, an expensive smell. "I like meeting my sister's friends."

"I will," Gerald says. "I've enjoyed myself so. I've heard so much about you."

"I didn't get to see my Charlie," Judith says, leaping into the breach. "I miss my good-night kiss."

"Next time he'll be up."

"Stay out of trouble," Elliot says to her, and then he turns to give Gerald a firm handshake, mano a mano.

She shares a cab home with Gerald, each to their own little lairs, even though they live in opposite directions. She leans against his corduroyed arm, relieved to be heading out of Rebecca and Elliot's well-oiled domain and into the misplaced atmosphere of her own life.

"Was it unbearable?"

"Not at all," Gerald says.

"I wish I could be more like them."

"No you don't."

"I do."

"Then we probably wouldn't be friends."

"Yes we would. I'd be like them, only better. More open. Less smug."

"Your sister," Gerald says carefully, "isn't really like them."

"I know," Judith says. "But she married Elliot."

"He has a hearty laugh, I'll say that for him. And good taste in art."

Judith laughs. "My sister is actually the one who picks the art. She's very informed, goes to museums and galleries all the time. I thought one of those women had fake teeth, didn't you? They had such an unnatural gleam whenever she smiled."

"Definitely," Gerald says. "The one whose husband had been divorced."

"They looked good. Her teeth. Maybe I should do that to mine."

"Let me see," Gerald says. "Say cheese."

"Cheese."

"They look fine. We never talked about your true love."

"My true evil love."

"Are things okay?"

"No."

"You want to come up and talk?"

"No, but I appreciate the invitation."

He leans over and gives her a kiss.

"Thanks for the lift. It was out of your way."

Gerald stuffs some bills into her hand and then climbs over her. When he's closed the door of the taxi she gives the driver Howard Rose's address.

DIGRESSION #5

I KNOW I've asked you this already, but I'll ask again, it's a free country: What's *your* sex life like? Did you get to marry the girl or boy of your wet dreams? And the wedding? Was it done with due ceremony, champagne and caviar, or did you opt for something more maverick, less cost-be-damned? If a bride isn't beautiful, they call her radiant, have you ever noticed that?

"Bill, I love you so / I always will . . ." Surely you remember Laura Nyro, circa 1970s, one of those waif songbirds who enjoyed a brief soaring fame. She was rumored to have been involved with David Geffen early in his career when he was still trying sexual predilections on for size. Sometimes it seems as though anyone who can't make up their mind about sex moves sooner or later to California.

The authoress is full of rueful musings today, isn't she, stuck in New York on a bright June day, with her own wedding dress hanging somewhere in the back of a closet, worn once, yellowing. It's in the nature of wedding dresses to be worn once, of course, but you'd think that fact alone would raise the alarms. And your wedding dress, tell me about it, send me a photo: Encrusted with pearls, was it, or worked with lace, shirred or Empire, country-girlish or siren-womanly? Is it yellowing somewhere along with all the other wedding dresses, collecting the earmarks of age without in fact ever aging?

So it is that the authoress asks her reader: How old are you inside, underneath the collected earmarks of your chronological age? The notion of youth being wasted on the young is not merely a conceit of George Bernard Shaw; it's one of the most painful of human paradoxes. Time, for instance, is infinitely malleable in second grade, when you're sticking a flattened blob of Silly Putty on a frame of a comic strip and then lifting it off to find a perfect copy on its underside—a homemade one-man Xerox machine. Time is still infinite in high school when you're daydreaming in Mr. Solomon's class, your chin in your hand, at your desk in the second row from the left, three desks down. When, I ask you, does time stop being infinite? In her head Judith Stone would always be in her early twenties, her big toe not yet dipped into the water, Howard Rose light-years away, not yet stumbled upon at a party she almost didn't go to. She has turned thirty at the beginning of October (not to worry, I haven't switched the facts on you), but tell me this: What age are you if you don't feel the age you are? Are you thirty if you don't feel thirty? How long, that is, do you get to assess the situation before the situation claims you?

The thing about fate is that at some point or other—indiscernible to any but the gods, laughing in their throned chairs up in the heavens, looking bearded and tall like the gods in a children's compendium of Greek myths—it will begin to close in, circling you with its gossamer chains, against which you will strain without result. As you are looking elsewhere, thinking, *I have time, I am young, there's so much I have to do*, the lyrics of a melancholy Cat Stevens song, fate will steal up and close the book on you, announcing: this is the story of your life, no irony intended.

I am trying to tell you the story of her life, leaving out such pieces that I think will bore you or that don't suit my larger artistic purpose. If you are wondering about the intersection of my life with hers—where the fictional ends and the autobiographical begins, tell the truth, will the real Howard Rose please stand up—I, who am she, would have to say: mind your own business, missy.

So where were we?

We left off the briefest of whiles back with Judith Stone leaving a Friday-night dinner at her sister's together with her friend Gerald and giving the cabdriver the address of the man known as Howard Rose. This, as you know, is a novel about a sexual obsession. I meant to write it years ago, but other things intervened. These tangents away from the main event grow shorter. For which you are grateful, I suppose. It's her you're interested in, not me, right? If I'd known that all along, I might not have bothered explaining myself to you. But now do watch carefully. Fate is closing in. Something bad is about to happen.

XXI

"WELL, WELL," he says, his tone not quite friendly, standing in the doorway in a short brown terry robe, his hair wet and combed back, looking vaguely Aztec.

"I thought I'd surprise you," she says.

He continues to stand behind the partially opened door, eyeing her. She hears music in the background, one of his beloved jazz selections, a laconic trumpet sidling its way across the scale.

"You're all dressed up," he says.

"I was at my sister's for dinner."

"The rich sister," he says mockingly.

"Yes. Howard, are you planning to let me in?"

"Maybe."

He opens the door a crack wider and continues to watch her, his head cocked to one side.

"Were you alone?"

"Where? Now?"

"At your sister's."

"Yes."

No point in explaining about Gerald. It would only invite some gratuitous comment about homosexuals in publishing or her faggy taste in general.

"I don't believe you," he says. "But do come in."

He holds the door after her and watches as she goes and sits on his couch.

"You're in a great mood," she says.

"I am," he says. "Or at least I was."

He sits on the other couch where his papers are, his long legs crossed under him, Buddha-like. Before he pulls his belt tighter, she catches a glimpse of his nakedness underneath the robe.

"Mind if I continue with my reading?"

"No," she says, although she does. "What are you reading?"

"Legal briefs," he says, marking something with a pen.

"Interesting?"

"To me."

She leans back and closes her eyes. The music sounds different to her with her eyes closed, more expressive and less laconic; the trumpet has been joined in its meanderings by a skittish piano, but they both sound as though they've lost their way. If she keeps her eyes closed long enough, perhaps he'll swoop down like magic upon her sleeping self.

"What'd you come here for?"

She opens her eyes.

He's put his papers down and is leaning back, elbows

outstretched, his head cupped against his hands. His robe has fallen open.

"I wanted to see you."

"What the fuck do you want from me that you can't get from one of your other boys? The ones you bring home?"

So that was it: he wanted to be included. He was hurt that she kept him apart from the rest of her life, although she thought she had been following his lead. All that "Do I own you now?" stuff, the two of them an island unto themselves, hadn't that been his wish?

"There aren't any other boys, as you call them. What are you so angry about? I came to see you."

"You didn't come to see me. You came for a fucking."

A fucking. He made it sound like a punishment. A punishment sounded good to her right now, better than what he was doing. If sex was the original sin—which is what she believed it to be, despite her own religion not recognizing the concept—clearly there should be some ritual devised to expiate the sinner. What was one to do with the need for punishment in a secular world? The childish wish to be absolved of adult imperatives such as lust apparently made perfect sense to the Catholic Church, where the need for penance had been met with great ingenuity via the option of confession: Bless me, Father, for I have sinned. But being Jewish was different; Jews prided themselves on giving short shrift to the atavistic, no messing around with wafers and wine for them.

"No, I didn't come for that. Howard, I don't know why you

always have to bring everything down to the lowest level. What would you say if I told you I missed you? That's really all there is to say."

"You missed my dick, that's what you missed up there on fancy Fifth Avenue."

Judith has grown up with the sense that you were supposed to figure out the repercussions of desire on some metaphysical level, work it all out in your head. But she couldn't work it all out in her head: Beat me, Howard Rose, for I have sinned. Why didn't he push her up against the wall, beat her black and blue, fuck her black and blue, bad girl that she was.

"It doesn't interest me to smack you around."

She is startled. How transparent had she become? Could he smell the moistness between her legs?

"It doesn't interest me," he is going on, reading her perverted Christian scenario as clearly as if it were written on her forehead, "or I would."

"Is that what was done to you?" She decides to take a detached tone, speak to the wounded inner child in him.

" 'Is that what was done to you?' " He repeats her question, mimicking her. "Spare me your psychology crap, will you. I'm talking about you."

"I see," she says.

What she sees is his prick, stiff and engorged, sticking out like a flag.

"I don't love you anymore," Howard Rose says.

"I see," she says again.

"You're a cunt," he says softly.

Why does being reduced feel so right—so exciting—to her, the disparity in power between a man and a woman, between herself and Howard Rose, displayed like a trophy?

"I'm going," she says, fighting back if only to prove to herself she wasn't really split in two, a grown fierce woman and a groveling knee-high girl. "I never want to see you again."

"Yes, you do," Howard says. "Because you love me. You love the way I feel inside you."

Get up, get up from the couch, Judith tells herself. Walk out and don't look back. Everyone makes mistakes. This one was yours . . . it must have gotten started long ago to have survived all the appurtenances of normality, this yen for humiliation; it must have been very strong to survive going undercover all day while she held her own in the office. It must have begun somewhere back in a garden behind the first summer cottage her parents rented on the Cape, the mosquitoes buzzing around her, a little girl watching her father water the flowers with a long green hose, a quick flick of his wrist on the nozzle and everything would bloom forever.

"Take off your clothes," he says. "Your rich-sister dress-up clothes. I want to see you naked. I think about your naked body during the day, did you know that? While I'm defending some jackass pervert killer, I'm really paying attention to your tits floating above me."

How, she wonders, has she managed to gravitate to this place, this dot along the time-space continuum that is Howard Rose's beige-and-brown apartment on a Friday night in November in the last quarter of the twentieth century? Could it be that there was something inherently wrong with her? Or was it erotic arrangements in general that were seriously flawed? Either dull and regular or thrillingly irregular, take your pick.

"I thought you said you don't love me anymore."

"I did say that. Because you made me say it. You can be a real cunt."

She feels on the verge of crying.

"I want you to crawl," he says. "I want you to crawl to me."

She suddenly thinks of Rabbi Klein, who wore *tzitzit* under his shirt and believed in the possibility of goodness. She is marooned with a savage, on a journey of her own making. How will she ever get back to the mainland, where people laugh, buy ice cream cones for their children, check out whether theater tickets are available? Uptown in Rebecca's apartment the windows face Central Park, where the trees are almost bared for winter, and in his room with the night-light in the shape of a duck, her nephew, Charlie, coughs and stirs in his bed. Her sister must be settling in, nestled against the sleeping back of her husband.

"Why?"

Someone is asking her to jump off a roof and all she wants to know is why, as though there is a logical answer. Behind the smell of sex is the smell of something rotten, like flowers gone bad. She wants to fall into a bottomless pit, an orgy of self-forgetfulness from which she'll never wake up.

"Show me how much you love me. I can see you want to. Crawl toward me and put my dick in your mouth. You can see how much it wants you."

His erection was still there, accompanying him as he walked

from the couch to the bedroom. He moved with his odd, loping grace; there was something almost balletic about the way he walked, as though under his tough talk beat the heart of a dancer, a dandy, a she-man . . .

"Do it," he says from his bed.

She might be in a movie, some flickering grainy creature on a screen; she might be a high-concept pitch—bookish, feisty woman falls for sadistic jerk—playing to a breathless audience, except that she was in Howard Rose's apartment and her servitude was voluntary. Around her were things she knew, props from real life.

"Okay," she says, pulling off her dress and pantyhose.

She gets down on the floor, first one knee, then the other. The music has stopped, the trumpeter has put away his instrument and gone off for the night; there is utter and complete silence. It has always amazed her, the impassivity of inanimate objects: not one of them, not his clock radio or his bookcase or his keys, splayed on a silver ring on the dining table where he dropped them, spring to her defense; not one of them shouts "You can't treat her like that!" or "Don't talk to her that way!" They were all little Switzerlands, determined to remain neutral.

"You still have your underwear on. Take it off. I want to see those big tits of yours swinging."

And now somehow she is naked, squatting on her haunches, and she is crawling toward him.

"Do you like it?"

She can't see his eyes, and she doesn't answer.

"I asked you if you like it. Answer me."

"I don't know," she says. But of course she knows, if only because her body tells her, banging away low inside of her.

"Of course you know," Howard Rose says. "You're a very knowing kind of girl under your innocent act. You may fool other people but you don't fool me."

She is heated up like an engine at full throttle, ready to take off at his touch. His penis beckons, rising smooth and straight. She is craven, would do anything to fill this ache for him.

"No," she says, standing up. "I don't like it."

He reaches out, strokes her buttocks, round and round, then slips his hand between her legs.

"Tell the truth," he says.

What was the truth? She is slipping in the mud, squealing with appetite at the trough of desire. Could it be that under everything—progress with all its mighty isms promising to bring light into shadowy corners, humanism, feminism, egalitarianism—there was nothing but this ancient prehensile grip upon her, this terrifying descent into darkness?

"Yes," she says.

"Yes what?"

If you admitted to the darkness, did that make it go away? Judith suddenly thinks of her favorite high school book, *Lord of the Flies*. Hadn't the angelic boys rapidly succumbed to the errant power of Jack, the bad apple among them, turning against the hapless, plump Piggy and chanting "Kill the pig"? Didn't they know what she knew, that aggression had a dazzle all its own, against which goody-goody boarding-school homilies didn't stand a chance? There was nothing to be gained by holding out.

"Yes, I like it."

He is pulling her close now, toward him, pushing her mouth on him, passing the power. Soon he will be inside of her with his glistening penis, turning her milky until she flows with him.

"I love you," Howard says softly, over her head.

She was a knowing girl, hadn't he said so? What she knows is that this isn't love, no matter how good it feels, no matter what he says. It is about something else—something to do with her long-ago wish not to exist as a separate person, whatever the cost. How far is she willing to go to coax a man unable to love, at least not in any recognizable sense of the word, into making an exception in her case? She sees herself at the end of a long tunnel, tiny and lost.

Later, in bed, she holds him more tightly than she usually does, coiling herself around him as if she can keep him with her by sheer force. She thinks of the famous black-and-white photo of John Lennon and Yoko Ono, the two of them naked, sitting intertwined, like interlocking pieces of a puzzle. How long had their symbiotic relationship lasted before it fizzled out and John had gone carousing in LA with a girlfriend handpicked by Yoko? Who had the upper hand there?

"Hey," Howard says, "I'm right here, baby girl. Everything's going to be all right."

XXII

"HI," SHE SAYS, her heart thumping in her ears, when he picks up after the third ring.

"Who is this?"

"Me," she says, shivering. "Judith."

"Aren't you supposed to be on a ledge right around now?"

She ignores the hostile intent of the question, the lethal distaste with which he regards her lurches into dark moods, the high drama of her emotional life. After that evening in November, when she thought they were bound together as a couple, things had taken a nosedive. He had floated the idea of a threesome, which she found not only threatening but inherently unappealing. What would she want with another man—or woman, more likely—in the picture? What had happened to their island of two? He kept coming back to the idea until finally one night she threatened to jump out the window if he went on about it. She didn't know whether she meant it but at the time she thought she did: What was there to anchor her to her life if

Howard Rose wasn't in it? In any case, it was a mistake to make the threat. After that he started calling her less and then, about two weeks ago, casually suggested that they take a break from each other.

It is eleven thirty on a Sunday night in late December. Judith Stone has known Howard Rose a little less than seven months—it has been six months, three weeks, and a day since the night she met him—but it might as well be centuries. He is a pyramid risen inside of her; she has labored like a slave in ancient Egypt on creating him, brick after brick, sweating as the sun goes down. She can no longer remember a time before him. Everything else has receded into the shadows: she can make out the dim outlines of friends and families, the Xerox machine outside of her office, a half-full Styrofoam cup of coffee on her desk, someone wanting to talk to her about something urgent, but it's all so far away.

"What do you want?"

His voice is curt and clipped, a high wall meant to keep her off the property. She is standing in a phone booth several blocks from his apartment, to which she has taken a cab from her apartment. Earlier in the evening the temperature had dropped and there are scarcely any people out on the street, just a lone woman going by, bunched against the rawness, carrying bags from the A&P.

"I want to see you," she says, leaning against the booth for support.

"Forget it," he says.

"Please," she says.

"I said forget it. *Comprendes?*"

"You don't have to be mean about it," she says. "I think it's starting to snow."

In the headlights of a passing car, she can make out flurries falling. They look unreal, like the slanted lines depicting rain in a child's drawing. She feels unreal herself, pursuing a man who doesn't want her except as a caprice, a puppet to perform according to his manipulation of the strings. She has finally started seeing a new therapist, an earnest but not uncomprehending woman who wears red glasses, with whom she spends session after session parsing the whys and wherefores of her masochistic streak, her obsession with Howard Rose.

"Wear gloves," he says, then, softening: "Where are you, anyway?"

"Out in the cold," she says. "Near your apartment."

"Go home," Howard says.

"I can't."

"Sure you can," he says genially, as though he were talking to a frightened child.

"Howard—"

"Look," he cuts in, "I've gotta make this short."

"Howard, I need to see you."

He is silent on the other end of the line. How can she explain to him that it hurts, not feeling his warm body for days at a time. After the first real fight they had, at the very beginning, he had actually bought her a present: a glass heart hanging on a gold chain, the kind of pendant you could buy in a subway kiosk for a couple of dollars. And once, he had given her a bunch of flowers in cheap white paper printed with violets. The presents struck her as mockeries of the real thing, less because of the lack of expense than because of the lack of imagination. Still, their very inadequacy made her feel oddly sorry for him—as though underneath all his womanizing banter no one had taught him the first thing about courting women.

"I need to see you," she says again.

Her heart is glass: surely he can see through it, the way it's splintered. It was the kind of situation that produced eloquent musical renditions of heartache but in real life you could hardly talk about, you just went mute and hoped someone would tend to your anguish.

"I can't," he says.

"Why not?"

"You don't want to know. Anyway, I'm not good for you. Everyone's always telling you that, right? Go find someone who's good for you while there's still time."

"I don't want to," she says, almost whimpering. Judith looks out and notices the snow beginning to form the thinnest carpet on the pavement. She imagines herself leaving the phone booth only to be found, buried under white mounds, in the morning. He will weep when they dig her body out, his tears will fall over the frozen strands of her hair, the very hair he once ran his hands through when she lay over him, breasts dangling. *Do I own you now?* No one has wanted to own her before Howard Rose, maybe that was the problem.

"There's someone here," he says, and then the recorded message cuts in, telling her to insert more coins.

"Don't hang up," she shouts into the phone, fumbling for change. She lets the receiver dangle from its cord as she looks in her wallet. When she picks it back up, she says "Howard?" He doesn't answer her, and she says his name again, urgently: "Howard."

"What do you want?"

"Is there really someone there? I don't believe you. I don't believe you," she repeats.

She is talking to him through tears, years have fallen away and she is a little girl who wants Howard Rose to kiss the boo-boo and make it go away.

"You felt so good," he says softly, putting her in the past tense as though she were dead. "But you fucked up."

How had she fucked up? By inducing him somehow to say he loved her? Hadn't she crawled across the floor for him, demonstrated she was willing to pay the cost of his love—or whatever it was. But what would she do without him, without his laser focus on her sexual pleasure?

"I'm coming up," she says. "Please can I come up?"

She is afraid of him, the whiplash of his rejection.

"It must be cold, standing out there," he says. "Your nipples must be nice and hard."

She knows he's lying in bed, snugly under the covers. He's almost always in bed before eleven thirty.

"I'm coming up," she says again, and then adds boldly: "I know there's no one up there."

He chuckles into the phone. Tomorrow at the office she will have blue circles under her eyes but there will be nothing else to indicate that she has stood on a street corner close to midnight, in a phone booth with the snow falling outside, her dignity crumpled up like one of those pink message slips that pile up on her desk, to be fished out of the wastebasket by the cleaning woman at the end of the day.

"Say it," he says.

"Say what?"

"You know. Say it or I'll hang up."

Who is she? And where are the men in white to save her from herself?

"I want to fuck you," she says.

"Say it again," Howard Rose says, "quick."

"I want—" she says.

"What?" He breathes into the phone, she can feel his tongue in her mouth. "What do you want?"

"To fuck you."

"Do you? Maybe you should have thought of that sooner."

She stands there, winded, as though someone had punched her in the stomach. All this back-and-forth only for him to end up denying her, banishing her into oblivion. When will she get the message? He has no use for her. Game over. She is still pondering the impossibility of it when she hears a click on the other end of the line.

Sobbing wildly, Judith stands in the phone booth, debating her options. She could try calling him back and seeing whether he might soften up, but she has grown tired of demeaning herself—maybe her sessions with the new therapist were getting through to her, after all. Or she could throw herself under an oncoming subway car, like a modern-day Anna Karenina, be rid of all that ails her and hope for a better life the next time around. The idea of ending it all has always drawn her but the finality of it frightens her—the thought of never having another late-night conversation with Celia, or another brunch with Gerald, or never seeing her nephew, Charlie, again, with his giggly pleasure at being tickled, makes her sad.

Or, again, she could try to do the unthinkable and move on, try to face up to her demons, wherever they came from, with the help of her therapist instead of acting on them. It would take a certain willing suspension of disbelief on her part—she had always liked that phrase and who said she couldn't apply it to her own reality just as well as to other people's novels?—but it might be worth a try. She exits the phone booth and pulls on a pair of suede gloves with a cashmere lining she had sprung for at Barneys. She suddenly feels complete, less vulnerable, an adult woman who looks out for herself.

It is snowing in earnest now, soundless and white. Judith sees a lone taxi inching its way along, miraculously free, its headlights picking up the swirls of snow, and puts up her hand. The driver zigzags to a halt. She settles inside the warm cab for the ride home; at the first red light the driver, a gentle-looking man in a knit cap, turns around.

"It's treacherous out there tonight," he says, "but you're in safe hands."

XXIII

FINALLY, THOUGH, it must be admitted, I don't know how to make you see Howard Rose as I saw him. How to capture for you the effect he had on my limbic system, sending it into disarray almost on cue. The problem with writing about sex, of course, is that the proper parsing of the manifestations of desire and arousal remains outside—beyond—language. None of which is helped by the curiously limited vocabulary of erotic life ("throbbing," "dick," "wet," "limp"), ensuring that we each stay stuck in the glue of our own experience, the radical solipsism of it. The experience remains opaque, untranslatable, radically subjective. It seems to me that this has always been the case, except in times of great repression, when the very words for relevant parts of the body—"tongue," "mouth," "thigh," even "ankle" (see *Madame Bovary*)—seem to swell on the page, leaking their juice. In times like ours, where everything goes, you run up, sooner rather than later, against the limits of the available terminology. The erotic becomes comically pornographic before you can say "He took me in his arms and kissed me."

How do other people let go? I've never understood it, although God knows I've tried. I connect this inability to a basic lack of hope in myself. Who will ever want me again after this rejection? Or, more to the point, whom will I ever want? In a way, it is a yawning gap in my survival mechanism. There is a rock in my path and instead of walking around it, I pick it up and say, "Rock, I love you. Please will you love me back."

There are clues that there are other people out there who have difficulty with this as well—mostly women, of course, but also a few highly sensitive men. I read in a biography of François Truffaut that after his affair with Catherine Deneuve ended, he sank into a deep depression for months in which he did little else but sit by the phone, waiting for her calls. He eventually went for a sleep cure, and seemed to have come around, continuing to make movies and to have relationships with other beautiful actresses. I'd always been fond of Truffaut's films, but when I read that detail I felt less lonely and uncontemporary in my sorrow. I thought of one of my favorite Truffaut movies, *The Story of Adele H.* I loved that movie, with Isabelle Adjani playing Victor Hugo's besotted daughter, in her long, sober nineteenth-century dresses, unable to give up on a delusional romantic connection with a British soldier who was briefly stationed with his garrison in Halifax.

But in our day, or haven't you noticed, everyone seems to get over everything very quickly, except for a few misfits who stalk women, and women who are attracted to men who destroy them. Then there are those rarer types who flourish inside obsessions, who draw their oxygen from its fetid, claustrophobic atmosphere, its mangled notion of loyalty. Types such as Baudelaire, who wrote a letter to a courtesan he had admired from a distance over many years in which he proclaimed that "fidelity is one of the signs of genius."

Meanwhile, the years have passed. At some point in my late thirties, I became tired of polishing other people's sentences and left book publishing to try to pursue my own writing. Then there is Richard and Sarah—and the fact that I am eight months pregnant, my belly big and taut.

"I don't get this," Richard says. He is reading something in a section of the *Times*, the one weighty with ideas and opinions, frowning.

"Don't get what?"

I am looking at an issue of *Vogue* that's several months old and wondering why I torment myself with these slinky bodies and photogenic faces attached to models whose names I actually know, as though it were vitally important.

"Oh, I dunno. I do get it, I just don't agree with it."

Richard is a radiologist, used to having abstract conversations with photographic images, X-rays, CT scans, MRIs, and the rest. What are you hiding? Is that a tumor in disguise? Or just a healthy little irregularity posing as an alarming deviation? It's an art form all its own, I suppose, this endless teasing out of shadows and light, calibrating the subtle patterns of disease, but it makes for a certain annoying indirection when it comes to human discourse.

"You're not reading that idiot again," I say. "You never agree with him, but you read him anyway."

"I like having my opinions confirmed," he says, reaching for his coffee, which he habitually lets cool until it's tepid.

It is a Sunday morning, late, and Sarah toddles on wobbly legs toward me, wearing pink overalls that are on the cusp of being too small for her. I can still smell her freshly shampooed hair, that fine and glossy baby hair, a color she got from God knows where, a shade like burnt caramel, worthy of Titian's palette. People would stop me on the street when she was little, swinging her legs in the stroller, and marvel at the glory of that hair, and I would pause and smile, like a proud L'Oréal technician, as though I had personally mixed up vials of yellow and red and gold dye to produce the desired effect. My pumpkin, I call her, for no reason at all. I watch her with her dolls, how she clutches them, then puts them down without looking back. Maybe that's why she is more casual with me than she is with her father. I am a grown-up version of her dolls while Richard is the Other, the grown-up to be wooed, to be anxiously kept in view even when he is lolling on the floor. "Daddy, Daddy, come, show you," she says.

Outside it is gray and drizzly. Melville wrote about a "November in my soul," a phrase I read in one of my college classes that has stayed with me. But it is March weather that I truly dread. Inside there are dishes with traces of scrambled eggs in the sink, other dishes with toast crumbs. We are a man and a woman and a child—a nuclear family, they call it—in a too-small apartment in a city I keep promising myself I will leave one day.

"Miss Sarah," Richard says, getting up from the table and pretending to peer around corners. "Where's Miss Sarah?"

She hides behind me, giggling. I absently stir my half-empty cup of tea, trying to mentally track down the source of my anxiety. It could be anything: the day itself, I've always hated Sundays, especially the late afternoon, when everything seems to be coming to a close; a preschool appointment I'm dreading in which I will be called upon to act the official role of overeager mommy, one mother among many other official mothers; my marriage, which makes me grateful and restless in equal parts.

The last time I felt no anxiety was—was when? When I was lying on my back with Him: Him, whom I weaned myself from because he was the sort of man who made no sense if you were planning to live a life with a real narrative structure, a beginning that looked to a middle that smiled upon an end. Who made no sense, in other words, if you knew how to distinguish between yourself as a tragic character—Emma Bovary by way of Anna Karenina by way of *9½ Weeks*—and yourself as a flesh-and-blood person beyond the reach of even the most gifted novelist.

Didn't I have a headache that day? Strange, the way my life keeps happening in the present tense even as it moves along from a past that hasn't yet fully registered into a future that is about to happen—like one of those trick shots in the movies where two people are talking in a car that isn't really moving but is made to look as if it is by the changing scenery rolling alongside it.

Narrative demands chronology, I know that, without it you might as well be tossing off a poem. The reader has a right to know when these things happened, and how many years have passed, not to mention where, and what about this child she's talking about, this Sarah. What can I say? Maybe this isn't a novel but an approximation, the best I can do under the circumstances. And then there is this: my feelings recognize no chronology. I know what you're thinking, such a female preoccupation, this matter of feelings. No wonder men—the proper globe-striding men who write for *The New York Times*, the men who run the governments that never quite work—don't read novels. The whole mad world seems constantly about to come crashing down, regimes topple overnight, flies buzz around the eyes of a starving child somewhere off in a hot, ravaged country, and women want to explore their feelings.

Meanwhile, Sarah is growing up, although I still call her "pumpkin" when I forget that she's too old for such nicknames, I still count the smattering of freckles across her nose and cheeks, and I still say "There you are" when she comes in the front door with Maria, our babysitter, as though she's just back from the North Pole and my hair has turned white. She often sleeps in our bed, although I recognize she is too old for this, certainly from a strictly psychoanalytic perspective. After all, I am not living in a primitive culture, like Papua New Guinea—the kind Margaret Mead studied and apparently got all wrong, or not right enough, according to the rigorous, avowedly non-Eurocentric viewpoint that is the gold standard in anthropological studies these days. But it's precisely the absolute unselfconscious aspect of those cultures, the sheer instinctiveness of them, that I like. The idea of a bare-breasted mother carrying a baby around strapped to her back in a papoose as she sat stringing beads or sifting flour into a big wooden bowl that would sell for a fortune in a crafts museum today makes complete sense to me, a way of keeping both mother and child company.

Years before I had Sarah—before I had met Richard and before she was so much as a speck on the sonogram's screen—I would sometimes go and sit in the playground on weekend afternoons, over on the East Side if I didn't feel like walking and closer to Fifth Avenue if I did. Something about the bright, hopeful circus of playgrounds drew me—all those children yelling, up and down the slides, in and out of the sandbox, the mothers and housekeepers and an occasional starched nanny standing by attentively or languishing on a bench. From an adult perspective, it's like entering a closed world in which everything but the immediate crises of childhood are temporarily suspended: what matters is how high you can swing and if that little boy with dark hair has snatched your pail. There is always a bully and there is always a tentative girl of about six or seven who seems destined for a future at the end of which is nothing very promising.

I used to sit and watch, shielded by a book so as not to look unduly out of place like a female Humbert Humbert, and a great sadness would overtake me within fifteen or twenty minutes. It had something to do with observing the laws of nature at work, how early everything starts and how implacably everything keeps on going once it gets started. I suppose you could say I was thinking of myself under cover of musing about the world, and undoubtedly there'd be some truth to it. The question of who I might have been if things had been easier—better—has consumed me for much of my adulthood. I think it's a question that consumes a lot of people, actually, if they only knew it. All that lost potential washed down the drain of human life, with only once in a while a flare going up and there in the center is someone doing something miraculously well: a neurosurgeon, an Olympic skater, a medieval historian.

But there's also a part of me that has always been very curious, capable of watching a child who bears no connection to my life as he haltingly maneuvers his way around a jungle gym. In my head I give this little boy I'm watching a name, Harry, and when this Harry finally makes it to the top of the structure, where he stands for a moment in his apple-red duffel coat and surveys his dominion, I feel like standing up and giving him a hand. No one applauds us enough when we are young, I'm convinced of it, when we're still inclined to glow in response and haven't yet learned to feign the appearance of modesty, to smile in sheepish disclaimer: *Who, me?*

So, yes, I used to go to the playground before I was a mother, before I brought Sarah in her light blue snowsuit with yellow daisies, sitting in a stroller that she was anxious to get out of the minute we hit the park. There was something tonic about the sadness, then, because it came at me from far away, like an abstract concept; I didn't realize that it would be so hard to shake, that nothing would quite do it for me except the sort of man who was bad for me, a man I couldn't possibly hope to marry, a man like Howard Rose.

It has been years since I've seen him and he has become less real in the interval. (Sometimes I think I invented him from the beginning, that there was nothing to him, really, nothing as toxic as my own fantasy of the Rejecting Lover, the man who would destroy me if I hung around long enough.) Lately, though, he has resurfaced, like a virus, immune to my posturing, my impersonation of a well-adjusted woman living at some remove from the imperatives of heartache.

There are real-life diversions, of course, things that demand my attention. When I am helping my daughter with LEGO or admiring a drawing she has brought home from preschool or absorbed by a book or a movie or talking to Richard about our dinner plans for the following week, I forget. The rest of the time everywhere I look, I see him, behind my eyes. I walk around, remembering, trying to understand. Trying, that is, to master my bewilderment—why I was with him in the first place, and why I can't let go of him for good in the second. It's all implausible, except to the two for whom it made sense.

"He doesn't come up to your ankles," a man, a longtime acquaintance of his, once said to me. "He has nothing to offer you." It was an act of well-meant betrayal, I could see that. These comments were meant to be a compliment to me and a slur on him, but they had the opposite effect: How little you know him, I thought; I must rescue him from your misunderstanding, feature him in all his complexity until you see him as I do.

Why, you might ask, did I want to understand him? It's a form of archaeology, really, with me as the eager guide. See that man over there, the one who looks suspicious, like someone who will cause harm? Now if you look more closely, under that toppling pediment, you will see that he really is the injured party, a piece of him broken off long ago by someone careless. Or: you might think on first glance that the man seated across from you is icy cold, but if you study the curve of that archway, you will discern that he is smoldering inside, a furnace . . . It wasn't as though I didn't see him as others did: a man thirteen years older than I, still a bachelor at forty-two, with the kind of physical bearing that didn't make much of a splash. There was a tightness to him, a sealed-off quality, that gave no indication of his devouring nature. But I also saw him as the other half of me, someone damaged long ago, hoping that there might yet be a chance of being healed, of finding a blue clearing in the woods where he—we—would discover an oasis, a reprieve of sorts.

XXIV

A WEEK OR SO AGO I tried calling him again. It was right after the eleven o'clock news and something—something from way back that flickered for a minute up there on the TV screen in the set of a man's jaw—reminded me of Howard Rose. I let the phone ring, three, four, twenty times. I counted them: *twenty*. No voicemail, no answering machine, no display of that eagerness not to miss a message that I and everyone I knew exhibited.

I hung on with the receiver getting sweaty in my hand, willing him back, all the way back inside me again. But he was out, or more likely he was just not picking up the phone as a random exercise, just because he could. He was always drawn to that kind of thing—arbitrary tests of will, like Gordon Liddy—and I wondered whether he had been working late, as he occasionally did, composing a defense of some slit-eyed felon with an intricately worked-out legal argument of his own devising, or whether he was having a quick bite at his favorite coffee shop.

Or making love to some woman the way he had once made love to me.

I could feel myself swelling up just imagining his long, dry fingers tracing circles around someone else's nipples, imagining the getting-ready-to-fuck firmness of his cock. Nothing has ever meant as much to me—to my wish to be out of my own skin—as the milky-white lostness of sex with Howard Rose: it is an experience I've given up, for the sake of sanity, but have never lost sight of. In the end, you understand, it was a deliberate decision rather than a real change of heart; I don't think there is any other means of disentangling from this sort of tortuous passion than to reason your way out of it, over and over again, until something clicks and you realize you have confused the signals once again, mistaken the shadows for the light.

Still, I continue to wonder whether I am meant for this normal-looking life I strive so hard toward, the husband and child and the kitchen all cleaned up when the day is done. I hung onto the phone long enough to hear Sarah calling out in her sleep—but no, I was only imagining it—and Richard stirring next to me in the bed, caught up in a dream. After that I turned off the light on my side, felt a faint kick in my belly—more of a flutter, really—and lay listening to the sound of my own breathing in the dark.

ACKNOWLEDGMENTS

Heartfelt thanks to the friends who were early readers of my manuscript, who offered tweaks, suggestions, and moral support that were much appreciated: Jami Bernard, Patricia Burstein, Deb Garrison, Carol Gilligan, Una McGeough, Chip McGrath, Deborah Solomon, Susan Squire, and Claire Wachtel. Thanks also to my (mostly) patient and always wise editor, Ileene Smith, and her editorial assistant, Jackson Howard. Lastly, to my agent, Markus Hoffman, who is as generous with his time as with his insights.